Classic Fairy Tales

Classic Fairy Tales

ARCTURUS

storytime™

Text and illustrations © Storytime Luma Creative Ltd
www.storytimemagazine.com

Illustration credits

Betowers Illustrations: *Hansel and Gretel*; **Marga Biazzi**: *The Farmer and the Boggart*; **Gaia Bordicchia**: *Fate Finds a Fish*; **Livia Coloji**: *The Three Fishes*; **Aurore Damant**: *Three Little Pigs*; **Cathy Delanssay**: *Aladdin and the Magic Lamp, Cinderella*; **Ariane Delrieu**: *The Magic Porridge Pot*; **Valeria Docampo**: *The Snow Queen*; **Agnès Ernoult**: *Diamonds and Toads*; **Rodrigo Folgueira**: *The Three Wishes*; **Alessandra Fusi**: *Sleeping Beauty*; **Christelle Galloux**: *The Twelve Dancing Princesses*; **Anna Gensler**: *The Proud Peacock*; **Isabella Grott**: *The Fire Fairy*; **Florence Guittard**: *The Princess and the Pea*; **Anja Klauss**: *The Mermaid of Zennor*; **Sarah Kronborg**: *The Fairy Bride*; **Nan Lawson**: *East of the Sun and West of the Moon*; **Katya Longhi**: *Rapunzel*; **James Loram**: *The Monkey and the Crocodile*; **Anne-Marie Hugot**: *The Children of Lir*; **Martuka**: *The Little Mermaid*; **Melanie Matthews**: Cover Illustration; **Richard Merritt**: *Rumpelstiltskin*; **Audrey Molinatti**: *The Snow Child*; **Michelle Ouellette**: *The Frog Prince*; **Line Paquet**: *Thumbelina*; **Catherine Razinkova**: *The Little Fir Tree*; **Brad Renner**: *Jack and the Beanstalk*; **Margaux Saltal**: *Fairy Ointment*; **Daniel Shaffer**: *The Golden Staff*; **Flavia Sorrentino**: *The Clever Queen, Snow White and the Seven Dwarfs*; **Laura Sua**: *The Changelings*; **Ishan Trivedi**: *The Hedley Kow*; **Axelle Vanhoof**: *The Greedy Fox*; **Ana Varela**: *Atlanta and the Golden Apples*; **Aleksandar Zolotic**: *The Magic Gifts*.

ARCTURUS

This edition published in 2018 by Arcturus Publishing Limited
26/27 Bickels Yard, 151–153 Bermondsey Street,
London SE1 3HA

ISBN: 978-1-78428-924-9
CH005641NT
Supplier 29, Date 0618, Print run 7270

Printed in China

Contents

The Princess and the Pea

Once upon a time, there was a prince in a faraway kingdom who longed with all his heart to marry a true princess—one who had not just a royal name and royal blood, but a good, kind heart too.

The prince's search for such a princess had seen him travel all over the globe, without any success.

"Oh, there's no shortage of princesses," he complained to his mother, the queen, "but I've yet to meet a true one!"

The queen sighed. She had bought a new hat and was growing quite impatient to wear it to a royal wedding.

"What about Princess Octavia of Caravel?"

"Too stuck-up!" said the prince.

"Princess Velda of Vimheiser?"

"Too vain!" said the prince.

"Princess Eulalia of Fopland?"

"Too unkind!" cried the prince.

Just then, a mighty peal of thunder echoed all around the throne room. While the prince and the queen had been chatting, a huge storm had been brewing outside.

The prince stared glumly at the rain through the window, wondering if he would ever meet his true princess.

Suddenly, there was a loud knock at the castle door. The head footman appeared moments later in the throne room and announced:

"Your Majesties, may I present to you Princess Meribel of Merina."

Into the throne room stepped a young woman who was utterly bedraggled by the wind and the rain. Her hair was stuck to her face, her dress was soaking wet and water poured out of the tops of her shoes.

Though her clothes dripped a huge puddle on the floor, she elegantly curtseyed before everyone.

With a smile that lit up the room, she spoke. "Your Majesties, my entourage and I were journeying back to Merina when my carriage was struck by lightning. If you would be so kind, please could you accommodate us for the night until this fearful storm has passed and my carriage is repaired? My father, King Gallant, would be most grateful."

Though the young lady was a sorry sight, the prince was most impressed by her grace and good manners.

"Could she be a true princess?" he thought, as he smiled at her dreamily.

The queen, however, had other ideas—she felt quite suspicious of the soggy stranger and didn't believe her to be a princess at all. So while the king and prince fussed over their new guest, offering her clean clothes and warm blankets, and arranging something for her to eat and drink, the queen crept out of the throne room and into one of their guest chambers.

There, she instructed her maids to fetch twenty thick mattresses and twenty thick quilts. While they were gone, the queen placed a single pea on the bedstead.

The maids were rather puzzled by their instructions, but they piled the twenty mattresses and twenty quilts on top of the pea, and brought in a tall ladder so that the princess could climb up to the top.

When Princess Meribel saw where she would be sleeping, she was thrilled. She had never slept on such a magnificently tall and comfortable bed before and she was looking forward to a good night's sleep.

"What a wonderful bed!"

she exclaimed.

However, when the princess came into the throne room the following morning, her eyes were tired and red, and she couldn't stop yawning.

"Didn't you sleep?" asked the prince, feeling concerned for his guest.

"I'm terribly sorry to say that I have hardly slept at all!" said Princess Meribel. "You have been such kind hosts and I don't wish to be rude, but there was something dreadfully hard in my bed and I am black and blue with bruises. I thought I should let you know, so that other guests don't suffer as I did."

At this, the queen clapped her hands with excitement.

"My dear," she said to the prince. "This is your true princess!" And she told them all about the hidden pea.

"You see," she explained, "only a true princess is sensitive enough to feel a pea through twenty mattresses and twenty quilts! I do hope you will forgive me, dear girl."

Princess Meribel did forgive her. In fact, she even made a point of saying how nice the queen's hat was on her wedding day to the prince.

As for the pea—well, that was placed on a purple velvet cushion in a glass case, and put on display for all to see. Perhaps, one day, you will be lucky enough to see it for yourself!

Three Little Pigs

Once upon a time, there was a Mother Pig who had three little pigs—Pinky, Percy, and Curly. The three pigs grew up quickly and soon there was no room for them in Mother Pig's small house. She decided that it was time for them to go and seek their fortunes. She kissed them goodbye and wished them good luck.

"But, be warned!" she said to the three little pigs. "The wolf is big and bad, and he will try to trick you, and catch you, and cook you in a pie!"

The three little pigs, with knapsacks on their backs, set off down the country lane until they came to a crossroads. Each pig took a different direction.

Pinky Pig went east and walked along the road until she met a man trudging alongside a donkey with a huge bale of straw on its back.

"Please sir, can I have some of your straw to build my house with?"

The man was tired of walking and wanted to ride his donkey, so he gave Pinky the bale of straw. She thanked the man.

Nearby, she found a lush green meadow and built her straw house right in the middle. It was a square house with an arched door and two big windows.

A few days passed, then the sly wolf came by and knocked at Pinky's door. He licked his lips and said, "Little pig, little pig, please let me in."

But the little pig remembered what her mother had said and she replied, "No, no, no! Not by the hairs of my chinny chin chin!"

"Then I'll huff and I'll I'll blow your house

And the wolf huffed and he puffed, and he blew the straw house right down to the ground and gobbled up little Pinky Pig.

"Delicious!" said the wolf.

Meanwhile, the second little pig, Percy, had gone west. He walked until he met a man carrying a large bundle of sticks on his back.

"Please sir, can I have some of your sticks to build my house with?"

The man was glad to get rid of the heavy sticks, so he gave them all to Percy. Percy thanked the man.

Just down the road, he spotted a tall green hill and he built his stick house right on top of it. It was a round house with a round door and one window.

Soon, the sly wolf came by and knocked at Percy's door. He licked his lips and said, "Little pig, little pig, please let me in."

But the little pig hadn't forgotten his mother's warning. "No, no, no!" he said, "not by the hairs of my chinny chin chin!"

"Then I'll huff and I'll puff, and I'll blow your house down!" growled the wolf.

Soon, the sly wolf came by...

KNOCK! KNOCK!

And the wolf huffed and he puffed, and he blew the stick house right down to the ground and gobbled up little Percy Pig.

"Tasty!" said the wolf.

Meanwhile, the third little pig, Curly, had headed south. He walked until he met a man pulling along a heavy cartload of bricks.

"Please sir, can I have some of your bricks to build my house with?"

The man was worn out from pulling the heavy bricks, so he gave them all to Curly. Curly thanked the man.

He found a pretty wood, and built his brick house right next to the trees. It was a rectangular house with a tall door, four windows, and a chimney.

It wasn't long before the sly wolf knocked at Curly's door. He licked his lips and said, "Little pig, little pig, please let me in."

But the little pig remembered what his mother had said and quickly replied, "No, no, no! Not by the hairs of my chinny chin chin!"

"Then I'll huff and I'll puff, and I'll blow your house down!" growled the wolf.

And the wolf huffed and he puffed, and he huffed and he puffed, and he huffed and he puffed until he had no huff or puff left—and the brick house hadn't moved!

Curly peeped through the window and saw the wolf look up at his chimney with a sly smile. Quickly, Curly made a blazing fire and filled a large cooking pot with water. He put the pot on top of the fire to boil.

Just then, he heard the wolf scramble up the side of his house, patter across the roof, and squeeze down the chimney. *Whoosh!* went the wolf down the chimney and then *Splash!*—straight into the cooking pot.

Curly dashed over to the pot and put the lid on it, trapping the wolf inside. From that day on, the little pig lived very happily in his little brick house and was never bothered by big bad wolves again.

Cinderella

Once upon a time, there was a rich widower who had a daughter as happy and kind as could be. Though he loved his daughter dearly, he missed the company of someone his own age.

One day, he met a lady with two daughters. She seemed caring and nice, and they got along well, so he asked her to marry him. However, as soon as the wedding was over, the woman started to show her true nature.

She was cruel-hearted and mean and so were her two daughters—and they all bullied the man's daughter terribly. The stepmother was angry that the girl was more sweet-natured than her own daughters, and the two stepsisters were jealous of the girl's kind heart and beautiful face. Sadly, the widower died soon after marrying the woman, so the poor girl was left alone with them.

From that day on, the stepmother treated the girl like a slave and gave her chores to do from morning until night. The girl cooked all the food, washed the dishes, tidied the house, scrubbed the floor, and cleaned the chimney. The last job was so dirty that she was often covered in cinders, which is why they called her Cinderella.

The stepmother and stepsisters also made Cinderella wear a ragged dress and sleep on a bed of prickly straw, while they wore all the latest fashions and slept in fine four-poster beds.

Sweet Cinderella never complained, she just worked and worked until her hands and knees were sore—and every day was the same.

One morning, Cinderella's stepsisters let out squeals of delight—they had been invited to the palace ball. It was known that the king had a handsome son who was looking for a bride, so the stepsisters were very excited.

They spent the next week fussing and changing their minds over what to wear. This caused a lot of work for Cinderella, who had to make sure everything was perfectly ironed. Even worse, the sisters made Cinderella style their hair and do their make-up. This was no easy task, since no matter how hard she tried, she could not make her stepsisters look pretty!

One afternoon, as Cinderella was pinning and curling the youngest sister's hair for the third time, the sister teased, "Would you like to come to the ball?"

Cinderella let out a deep and sad sigh. "I would truly love to, but they would never allow me to enter wearing old rags like these."

"That's right!" said the younger sister in a sharp voice and both sisters laughed cruelly. Brave Cinderella held back her tears.

On the day of the ball, Cinderella rose before dawn so she could finish the housework, and help her stepsisters to get ready.
When at last they left, neither of them thanked
poor Cinderella for her help.

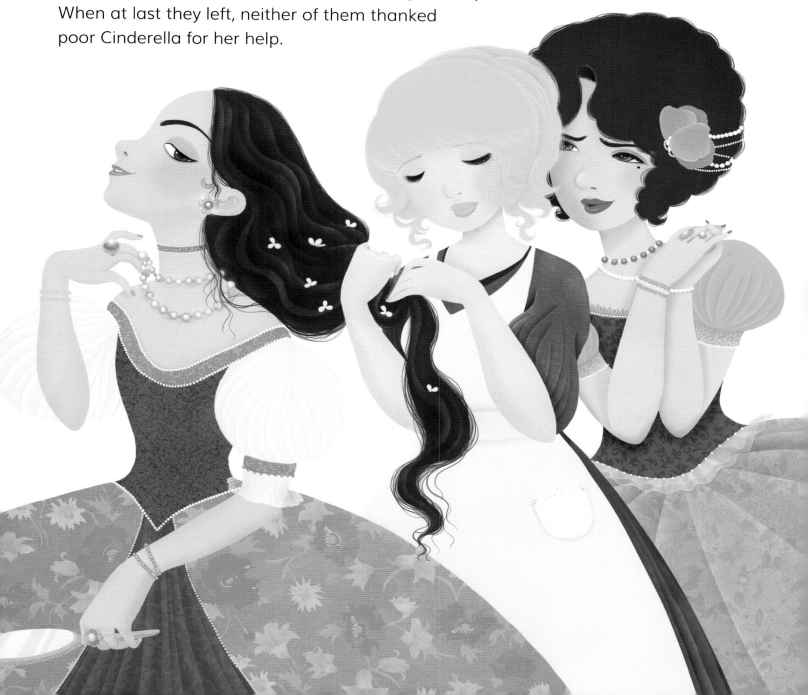

She watched their carriage disappear from sight, then sat by the fireplace and cried tears of true sadness. Suddenly, in the middle of her sobs, she heard a kind and gentle voice.

"Whatever is the matter dear?"

Cinderella saw, through her tears, a lady with sparkling eyes and the loveliest face she had ever seen. Cinderella tried to explain, but the tears kept flowing.

"Don't cry," said the lady in a soothing voice. "I understand. You wish with all your heart to go to the ball, but you can't. Is that right?"

Cinderella nodded woefully.

"Dear girl, I am your godmother and I promised your dear father that I would come to you when you needed me most. I think you need me now, so let's get ready for this ball."

Cinderella fell into her godmother's arms and hugged her—and then she remembered how she was dressed.

"But how can I go to the ball, when I have nothing but these dirty rags to wear?" cried Cinderella.

"Never mind," said the godmother with a reassuring smile. "Now run into the garden and fetch me a pumpkin."

Confused by such a strange request, Cinderella picked the finest pumpkin she could find. She placed it on the table and the godmother produced a splendid wand. She waved it over the pumpkin and instructed Cinderella to look outside. There, on the driveway, was a glimmering golden carriage!

"Now go to the mousetrap and fetch me six mice," said the godmother.

Cinderella did as she was told and lifted six little mice out of the trap.

The fairy godmother—for, of course, she was no ordinary godmother—waved her wand over the mice and asked Cinderella to look outside again. To her delight, Cinderella saw six dappled horses with shimmering silver manes.

"Now run into the garden and fetch me the lizard that hides behind the well," smiled the fairy godmother.

Cinderella quickly found the lizard and returned to her fairy godmother. Again, she waved her wand over it and, when Cinderella stepped outside, she saw a stylish footman sitting at the front of the carriage.

Cinderella could hardly believe what she was seeing, but when she looked down at her dirty ragged dress, her smile quickly faded.

"I haven't finished!" said her fairy godmother, and she touched Cinderella's dress with the wand, transforming it into a gown embroidered with gold and silver, and decorated with jewels that shone in the light. On her feet, Cinderella wore a pair of dainty glass slippers. Her hair was pinned up with tiny diamond clasps, except for a few ringlets falling around her neck. She looked beautiful.

"You shall go to the ball!"

said her fairy godmother.

Cinderella thanked her godmother and stepped into the carriage, her heart pounding with excitement at the prospect of the evening ahead.

"Before you go, Cinderella, you must promise that you will be home before the clock strikes midnight. The magic will stop working then and everything will be restored to how it was before."

Cinderella promised to leave the ball before midnight, and the carriage drove away led by the majestic horses.

When Cinderella reached the palace, news quickly spread of her arrival.

As she entered the room, everyone fell silent. The guests had never seen such beauty—they were enchanted. Even Cinderella's own stepsisters didn't recognize her. "How beautiful she is!" the guests whispered.

The Prince stepped forward and offered Cinderella his hand. They danced so gracefully, it seemed they had danced together all their lives. The night rushed by in a whirl of dancing, feasting, chatting, and laughter. Everyone was captivated by Cinderella's kind nature and she had never known such happiness!

In fact, she was having such a special night, that she forgot her fairy godmother's warning. In the middle of a wonderful dance, she suddenly heard the clock start to strike twelve.

Scared that the magic would wear off, Cinderella fled from the ballroom and ran down the palace steps as quickly as she could. In her haste, she left behind a single glass slipper.

Cinderella ran home, dressed in rags. When her stepsisters returned, they told Cinderella of the mysterious beauty who ran away at midnight and how the Prince had found her glass slipper. All night, Cinderella dreamed she was dancing with the Prince again.

A few days later, a royal guard sounded a trumpet in the town and announced that the Prince was searching for the mysterious beauty from the ball and would marry the lady whose foot fitted the glass slipper. The Prince's courtiers knocked on every door in the land, but had no success.

When, finally, the Prince arrived at Cinderella's house, her stepsisters tried to push and squeeze their large, knobbly feet into the dainty glass slipper, but it was no good!

One of the Prince's courtiers saw Cinderella peeking around the doorway and asked her to step forward. Her stepmother tried to stop her, but the courtier insisted.

Dressed in her rags, Cinderella sat before the Prince and gracefully slid her slender foot into the glass slipper. It was a perfect fit!

Her sisters were astonished, but the Prince was overjoyed—despite the rags, he knew he had found his true love. The fairy godmother appeared one last time and, with a wave of her wand, she dressed Cinderella in a gown fit for a princess.

Cinderella and the Prince were soon married in a magnificent ceremony— and, though her stepmother and stepsisters had been cruel to her, Cinderella invited them to live at the palace with her, because she was beautiful both inside and out.

Fairy Ointment

Many years ago, there was an old nurse called Goody who was known and loved by everyone for looking after the sick and helping to bring bonny new babies into the world.

One night, when she was tucked up in bed and ready for sleep, there was a loud knock at her door. Nurse Goody answered as quickly as she could and looked down to see a strange little fellow hopping nervously from foot to foot. He had pointy ears and a beard, and was quite clearly an elf of some kind.

"Madam!" exclaimed the elf. "My dear wife is having a baby and we urgently need your help!"

Before she could say a word, the elf took Nurse Goody by the hand and swept her onto the back of a horse that was as black as coal. He leapt into the saddle and they set off at such a fast pace that the nurse felt like she was flying through the air.

"Goodness!" thought Nurse Goody. "What kind of baby am I about to bring into the world? And where might this elf be taking me?"

But Nurse Goody was naturally very nosy, so she couldn't wait to see where they were heading—even if that place was somewhere magical.

Moments later, they arrived at their destination. The old nurse was rather surprised and a little disappointed to find that she was set down outside an ordinary-looking cottage on a hillside. She was even more surprised when she stepped inside and found an ordinary woman lying there. She wondered how the woman had come to marry someone from Fairyland!

As soon as she did so, the little baby stopped wailing and started to chuckle. She gazed around the room with wonder in her eyes.

"Hmm... I wonder what this ointment is for?" thought Nurse Goody. "Perhaps it's for tiredness? I feel quite tired now."

The old nurse's curiosity got the better of her. Ignoring the woman's warning, she quickly checked that nobody was looking, then smoothed a little ointment over her eyelids. When she opened her eyes, she was amazed at what she saw before her!

Suddenly, she could see that she was not in an ordinary cottage at all, but in the grand home of a fairy, with intricately carved furniture, fine silk fabrics, dancing butterflies, and a ceiling dotted with twinkling stars.

The mother, too, was far from ordinary—she was a fairy queen, wearing a

The nurse set about her work and very soon a healthy baby girl was born with a most powerful set of lungs. Oh, how the baby wailed! The new mother thanked Nurse Goody and gave her a small pot of ointment.

"She'll stop crying when she has this," said the woman. "Please smooth it over my baby's eyelids, but be sure not to put it near your own eyes."

The nurse thought it was an odd request, but as she was cleaning and dressing the baby girl, she did as she was asked, and gently smoothed the ointment over the baby's eyelids.

grand floral crown and a dress of shimmering midnight-blue satin. And the baby had two teeny fairy wings and pointed ears, just like its elfin father!

Nurse Goody knew then that the ointment was magical and it had the power to show things as they truly are. She was in Fairyland! However, she didn't let on what she knew, as everybody knows that fairies are secretive so, when the baby and mother were comfortable, she asked the elf husband to take her home.

They sailed through the air even faster than before...

The elf looked at her in shock, while everyone around the stall looked at the nurse in confusion.

"Can you see me?" asked the elf.

"Of course I can see you!" laughed Nurse Goody, quite forgetting about the magical ointment she had used.

"Argh!" shrieked the elf. "You used the ointment when my wife told you not to! Well, we can't allow humans to see us. I'll have to fix that right now!"

With that, the elf jumped up and touched the nurse's eyelids. When she opened her eyes, he had vanished from sight.

By now, a crowd had gathered round Nurse Goody. You see, only she had seen the elf, so they all thought she was talking to herself. From that day on, she became known as 'Nurse-Goody-who-talks-to-herself'—and she was never asked to help the fairies again. And that is what you get when you meddle with fairy magic!

As the elf whisked her onto the back of the black horse again, she could see this time that it had wings. They sailed through the air even faster than before and, when they reached the old nurse's cottage, the elf thanked her kindly and paid her generously.

A few days later, it was market day in town and Nurse Goody went along to do her shopping. As she approached the stalls, she spotted the elf husband filling up his basket with goods.

Nurse Goody walked up to him and tapped him on the shoulder.

"Good day to you!" she said. "How are your good wife and child faring?"

The Hedley Kow

In the village of Hedley-on-the-Hill in northern England, there lived an old lady who earned her living by running errands for people. She hadn't much money, but she was always cheerful and always had something good to say.

One evening, she was returning home after a long day's work when she noticed an old pot by the side of the road.

"Who could have left that there?" she wondered, and she looked around for its owner, but there was no one about.

"Well, I'm sure I could put it to good use!" she decided, and she hobbled over to pick it up. As she drew nearer, she saw something glinting inside it.

"Goodness me, it's full to the brim with gold pieces!" she cried.

She could hardly believe her own good fortune. "Oh, I do feel lucky!" she laughed. "I'll never want for anything again with all this gold."

The old lady knew that the pot would be too heavy to carry, so she tied her shawl around its handle and dragged it along the road behind her.

As she walked along she chuckled, "Why, I must be the luckiest lady in the world!"

It was hard work dragging the heavy pot and the old lady soon grew weary, so she stopped to rest for a minute. But when she checked on the pot of gold, she saw that it had turned into a huge lump of silver.

"Fancy that!" said the old lady. "I must have been dreaming. I was sure it was gold! Ah well, silver is even better— it will be much easier to keep it safe. How lucky I am!"

And she set off for home with a smile on her face, dreaming about silver.

It wasn't long before she needed to rest again, but when she turned to check on her treasure this time, she let out a cry of astonishment.

"Well, what about that?" she grinned. "Is that a great lump of iron I've been dragging behind me? I could have sworn it was silver! Well, my luck just gets better and better! No need to worry about being robbed now!"

And she set off down the road again, laughing at her own amazing fortune.

As she neared her front gate, she glanced back at the lump of iron to find another surprise.

"Ha! It's changed into a rock! How did it know that this is just the thing I need to hold my door open? What people would give to be as lucky as I am!"

The old lady couldn't wait to see how the rock looked by her front door, so she heaved it up the path as quickly as she could and untied her shawl.

But, just as she lifted the rock to place it near her door, it suddenly sprang to life and jumped out of her arms to reveal four strong legs, two pointed ears, and a long swishing tail. The rock had transformed itself into a brown and white cow!

The cow ran across the room, kicked its heels in the air, jumped through her window, and trotted down her garden path, laughing and mooing as it went!

"There's no doubt about it!" the old lady grinned. "This is my lucky day! Fancy me getting to see the famous Hedley Kow! Who else can say that? Why, I do feel grand!"

And the old woman went to bed that night feeling like the luckiest person in the world.

Diamonds
and Toads

Once upon a time, there was a mean-spirited mother who lived in the woods with her daughters, Selena and Amy.

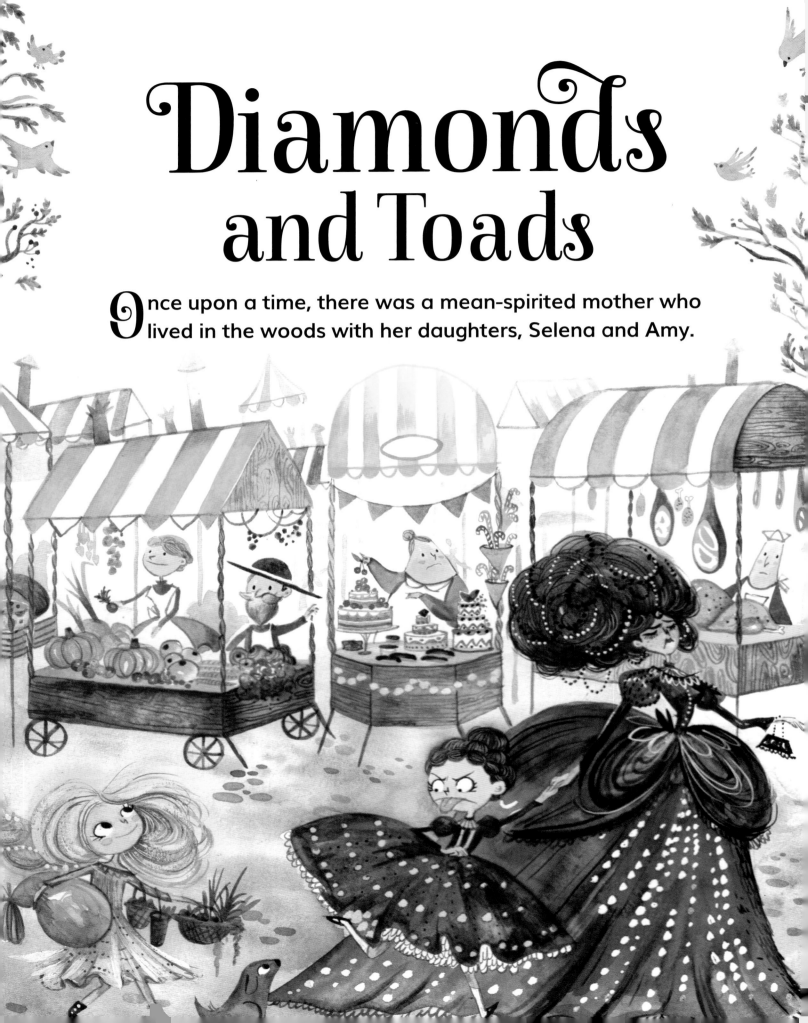

The elder daughter, Selena, was often mistaken for her mother since she looked and behaved so much like her. Her mouth turned down at the corners and she hadn't a nice thing to say about anyone or anything. She was also the laziest lump anyone could ever wish to meet. When Selena and her mother went to the local village on market day, nobody was glad to see them.

But the younger daughter, Amy, was adored by everyone. She had her late father's sparkling eyes and kind smile and, like him, she always treated everyone with respect.

When Amy was sent to the village by her mother and sister, as was often the case, everyone wanted to chat with her.

This drove the mother mad with jealousy. She loved the elder daughter, because they were so alike, but, in time, she grew to resent her younger daughter for being so nice and popular all the time. To punish Amy, she made her do all the chores and cook all the meals. Worst of all, she made her walk twice a day, whatever the weather, to a well far away in the woods and carry back two heavy pails of water.

Amy knew that her mother and sister were being unkind, but she hoped that one day, they would love her.

On a cold winter's day—cold enough to see your breath in the air—Amy was drawing water from the well when a frail old woman, wrapped in a ragged shawl, hobbled up to her.

"Please, young lady, can you spare me a drink?" asked the old woman in a trembling voice.

"Why, of course, madam!" said Amy. "Sit down here and I'll fetch some for you." Amy took off her shawl and wrapped it around the old lady's shoulders to keep her warm, then she held the pail of water to her lips so that she could sip from it.

"Are you warm enough now?" asked Amy. "Do you have somewhere to sleep tonight?"

When the old woman had finished sipping, she smiled at Amy and said, "Such kindness! What a lovely girl you are." Then the old woman pulled Amy's shawl over her face and, when she whisked it away, she had transformed into a woodland fairy, wearing a crown of forest flowers and leaves.

"I would like to give you a gift," said the fairy. "From now on, whenever you wish it, when you speak, diamonds and gems will fall from your mouth." And, with that, the fairy disappeared.

Amy wondered whether she might be imagining things, so she filled the two pails and heaved them home again. When she arrived, her mother scolded her for taking so long.

Amy closed her eyes and wished for jewels to appear, then she said, "I'm so sorry, Mother, but something wonderful happened at the well."

As she spoke, large diamonds

and gems fell to the floor!

"What is this?" cried the mother. "Where did you steal these from, wicked girl?"

Amy explained what had happened, scattering more precious stones as she spoke. The mother greedily scrambled around the floor, grabbing them, and shoving them into her apron pocket.

"Did you hear that Selena? Have you seen the luck of your wretched sister? You must go to the well too!"

Selena glared at Amy jealously, but said, "You want me to walk all that way? No thank you!"

"All you have to do is walk there and, when an old lady asks for some water, give her a drink!" wailed the mother, but Selena didn't budge.

The mother flew into a rage. "I'm not *asking* you to go, you lazy girl, I'm telling you to go this instant!" And she shoved Selena out of the house, calling after her, "And try to be nice!"

Selena loafed along lazily to the well, shivering all the way there—she wasn't used to being out in cold. When she arrived, she had just started to fill up a pitcher with water when a beautiful princess appeared.

"I'm so thirsty—please may I take a sip of your water?" asked the princess.

"No, you may not," said Selena with great insolence. "Do you think I've come all the way into this miserable, cold wood to be your servant? Why not get one of your slaves to do it?" And Selena tutted and huffed.

The princess smiled and, in that instant, she transformed herself into the same fairy Amy had met earlier.

"It is a pity you are not like your sister," she sighed. "But I will give you a gift. You'll see what it is later."

Selena shrugged and set off for home. "Perhaps I should have been a bit more polite," she thought, then she remembered the diamonds and jewels and she started to walk a little quicker.

When she walked through the door, her mother leapt up. "Well, how did it go? Did she give you a gift?"

Selena tried to answer, but her cheeks suddenly felt quite full. "Yes!" she said, and two toads fell from her mouth and plopped onto the floor.

Every time Selena tried to talk to her mother, more toads fell to the ground, until the floor was hopping with them.

The fairy had given the rude and lazy girl exactly what she deserved.

"This is your sister's fault!" cried the mother. And she ran off to the woods to try to find the fairy and remove the curse she had put on Selena.

That was the last the two sisters ever saw of their mother and, without her mean presence in the house, they eventually became best friends.

Amy used her gift to buy a wonderful house in the village and to help those in need and, in time, Selena learned that if she only said nice things, then no toads hopped out of her mouth. And, if a toad did appear, she took it to the pond, where it could live happily ever after!

Aladdin and
the Magic Lamp

In Persia, there once lived a poor widow who had a son called Aladdin. Sadly, Aladdin was a lazy boy who would daydream all day rather than help her.

One day, a wealthy stranger approached Aladdin on the street and claimed to be his long-lost uncle, but really he was a cunning magician.

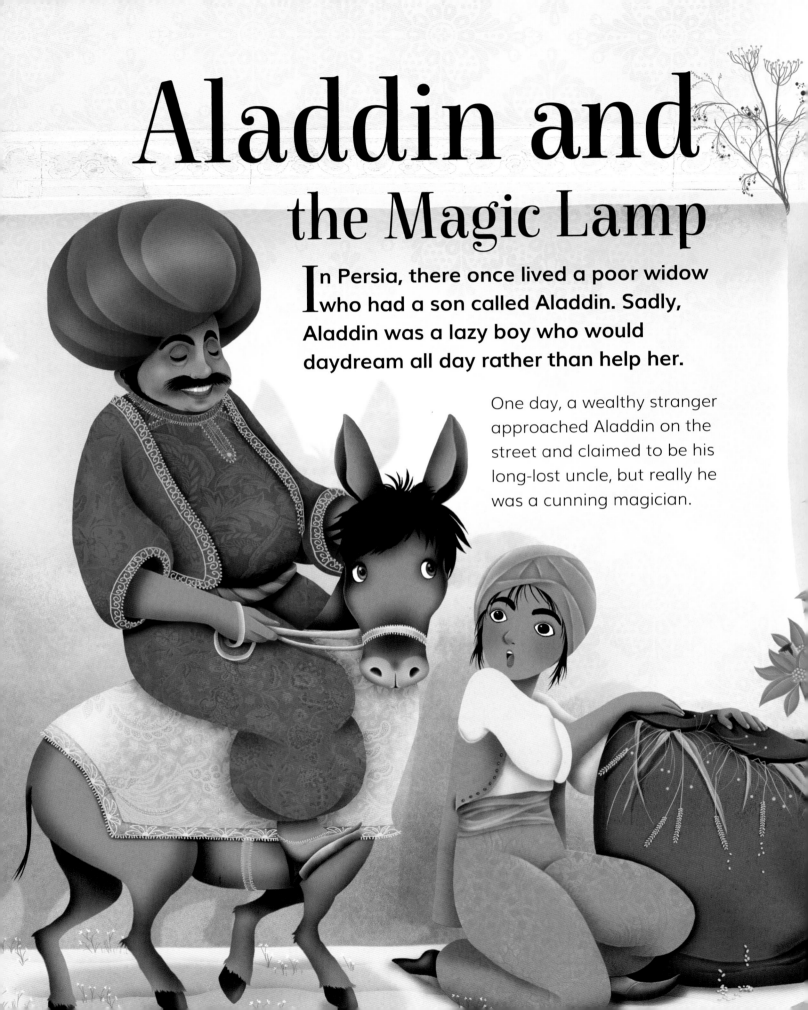

"Run home," urged the false uncle, "and tell your mother I am coming."

Aladdin quickly ran home, and told his mother the good news.

"Indeed," she said, "your father had a brother, but I thought he was dead."

When his uncle arrived, he came with gifts and grand stories. He explained that he had been out of the country, exploring the world for many years.

When he asked Aladdin his trade, the boy hung his head in shame, and his mother burst into tears. The uncle offered to look after Aladdin and he bought him fine suits of clothes, and showed him the sights of the city.

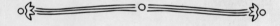

Soon, Aladdin's uncle asked him to join him on an important journey. He led Aladdin far from the city and deep into the mountains. Aladdin was tired and begged to go home, but his uncle led him on, telling him of his adventures.

They walked for many hours, until they reached a narrow valley. Here, his uncle said, "We will go no farther."

He pulled out a small velvet pouch from his robes and poured a strange powder into his hand. He threw it to the ground and muttered some magical words. "Now I will show you something wonderful," said his uncle.

The earth suddenly trembled and opened up before them, revealing a large, flat stone with a brass handle in the middle. Aladdin tried to run away, but his uncle grabbed him.

"You must do exactly as I tell you. Below this stone lies a treasure, which is yours, and only you may touch it."

He told Aladdin to pull open the stone, saying the name of his father. At the thought of treasure, Aladdin forgot his fears and pulled open the stone easily. Beneath it were some steps leading deep under the ground.

"These steps lead to three great halls. Walk through them without touching anything, or you will die instantly. At the end of the halls, there is a lamp. You must bring it to me."

Aladdin descended the steps, feeling quite afraid. As he entered the first hall, he could see piles of silver, sparkling brightly in the dim light. The second hall was better still—it was filled with glittering gold coins and crowns. But the final hall was best of all—it overflowed with jewels. Rubies, emeralds, sapphires, and diamonds were stacked so high that they towered over Aladdin. He could barely believe his eyes.

Though he was tempted to touch them, he remembered his uncle's warning and walked on until he came to a rusty old lamp. "Surely this can't be the treasure he means?" thought Aladdin, but he picked it up and carried it back to the cave entrance.

As he started to walk up the steps, his uncle shouted, "Throw me the lamp now, boy. Throw it up here!" His voice sounded quite anxious.

"No!" said Aladdin. "You can have it when I reach the top!"

"Don't be a fool, boy, throw it to me this instant!" his uncle shouted angrily.

Aladdin refused again. He was no fool—he had guessed that his uncle was just using him to get the treasure.

The cunning magician could see that his plan to get the lamp was foiled. He muttered his magic words and the stone rolled back into place. He trapped Aladdin and the rusty old lamp inside the cave with no way out, then he escaped across the desert.

Poor Aladdin spent two dark, lonely days in the cave trying to escape, but no matter how hard be pushed, the stone wouldn't budge. Shivering, he rubbed his hands against the lamp in despair and, as he did so, a large genie rose out of it, saying:

"I am the Genie of the Lamp, and your wish is my command!"

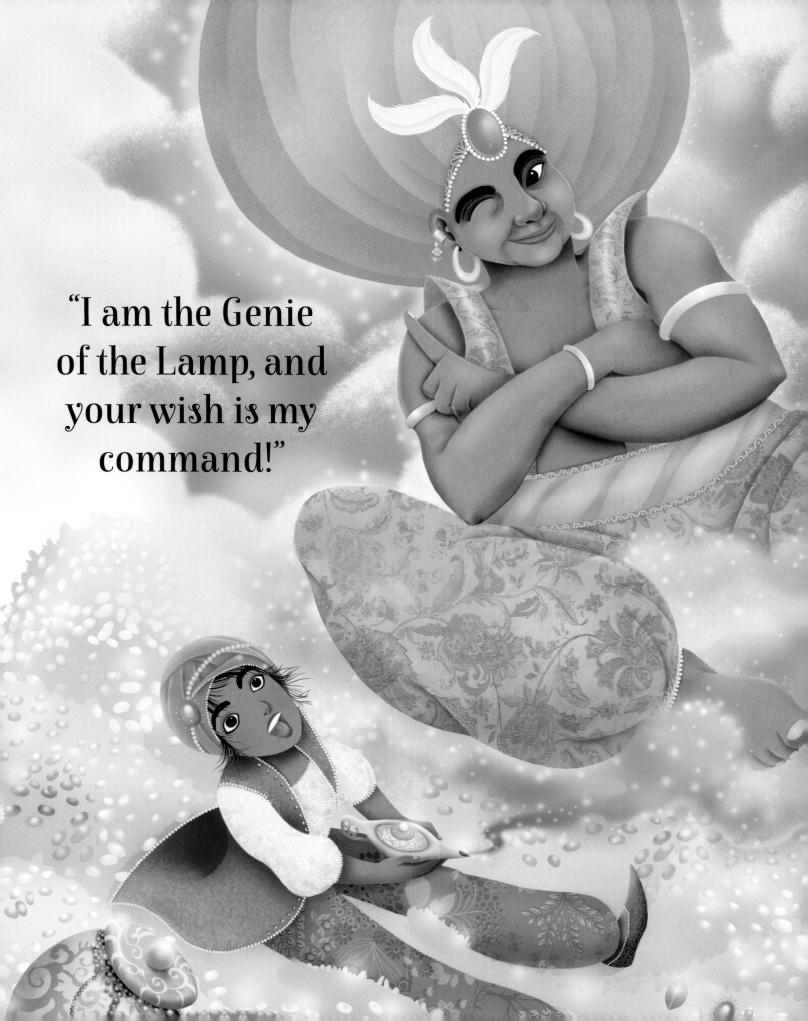

"I am the Genie of the Lamp, and your wish is my command!"

Aladdin was shocked, but he answered quickly: "Please take me home!"

There was a huge flash of light and, when Aladdin blinked open his eyes, he found himself at home beside his mother. He told her how the uncle was really a magician and had tried to trick him. Weak and hungry from his adventure, he begged his mother for some food. But his poor mother had nothing to give him.

Feeling bold, Aladdin rubbed the lamp and the amazing genie appeared again.

"I am the Genie of the Lamp, and your wish is my command!" he said.

"Please bring us something good to eat!" said Aladdin.

A second later, a grand table appeared with golden plates, bowls, and goblets, and a splendid feast of cakes, wine, and fruit—the likes of which Aladdin and his mother had never seen before. Aladdin's mother wept tears of joy.

From that day on, Aladdin and his mother were never poor or hungry again, for all they had to do was ask the genie for whatever they needed. And Aladdin was never lazy again—in fact, thanks to his magic lamp, his life was filled with many more exciting adventures, all waiting to be told on these pages.

The Three Fishes

In a great lake there lived three fishy friends called Think-Ahead, Quick-of-Wit, and Stuck-in-the-Mud.

One day, Think-Ahead was swimming along near the edge of the lake when she overheard some passers-by.

"Just look at all the fish in this lake!" they said. "Let's bring our boat here tomorrow and catch some for our supper!"

"This isn't good," thought Think-Ahead. "When these fishermen come back here tomorrow, we'll be in troubled waters. I must persuade my friends Quick-of-Wit and Stuck-in-the-Mud to find somewhere else to live or we'll all get caught in their nets."

She swam to her friends as quickly as she could and told them what she had heard.

"But I love it here!" said little Quick-of-Wit. "If the fishermen try to catch me tomorrow, I'll come up with a plan, just like I always do."

And Stuck-in-the-Mud sat on her rock and said, "Who's to say there won't

be more fishermen somewhere else? We don't know for certain that they will come back. I'm not moving!"

Think-Ahead tried to persuade her friends to escape, but their minds were made up, so she said a sad goodbye and swam to the other side of the lake, where she found a babbling brook to explore.

The next day, the two fishermen came back to the lake with an old rowing boat. They cast their rods and nets into the water and, as the day went on, they caught almost all the fish in that part of the lake.

As they hauled in a heavy net with Quick-of-Wit in it, the smart little fish decided to stay completely still.

"This one looks like it has been dead for days!" said one of the fishermen, and he threw Quick-of-Wit back into the lake. Quick-of-Wit wriggled away quickly, relieved to have escaped.

Meanwhile, Stuck-in-the-Mud refused to swim away even when she saw the boat arrive. She stayed in her shady spot at the bottom of the lake and got scooped up in the fishing net.

As she was lifted out of the water, for the first time in her life, Stuck-in-the-Mud regretted being so stubborn and wished that she had listened to her friend's advice. All too late, she realized why it is sometimes better to think ahead.

The Magic Porridge Pot

Once upon a time, there was a good little girl who lived with her mother in a tumbledown cottage in a village in the countryside.

The girl and her mother loved each other very much, but they had a hard life and very little food on their plates. They often wished for more to eat.

Every morning, to help her mother, the little girl would go into the forest to collect firewood and, if she could find them, she would pick a handful of berries for their breakfast too.

But one day, the girl found that the birds had eaten all the berries from the biggest bramble bush. The poor girl was so hungry, she began to cry.

A blackbird, which was perched on the bush, gave a loud squawk and, with a rustle of feathers, transformed itself into a forest fairy with long black hair and a cloak of black feathers. From beneath her feather cloak, the fairy produced a small black pot.

"Dear girl," said the forest fairy, "dry your tears. This gift will ensure that you never feel hungry again. When you need food," she told the girl, "just say 'Cook, little pot, cook!' and it will cook the tastiest porridge you have ever eaten."

She handed the pot to the little girl.

"And when you've had enough, just say 'Stop, little pot, stop!' and it will stop cooking for you. Now, can you remember that?"

The little girl nodded and thanked the forest fairy. Then she ran back to her mother as quickly as she could.

She burst through the door of their cottage, set the little black pot down on the kitchen table and cried, "Cook, little pot, cook!"

The magic pot started to bubble away and the cottage was soon filled with the sweet smell of warm porridge.

The girl's mother could hardly believe it, and the two skipped and twirled around the small black pot, before scooping the porridge into their bowls and eating it all up. The girl and her mother couldn't believe their luck!

From that day, every morning, they ate as much porridge as they liked—and when times were hard, they ate it for lunch and dinner too. They never grew tired of eating it, because they were so grateful for their magic porridge pot.

One day, when the little girl was out collecting firewood, her mother still felt hungry, so she decided to treat herself to an extra bowl of porridge.

She took out their magic porridge pot, put it on the table and said,

"Cook, little pot, cook!"

The mother scooped some porridge into her bowl and sat down to eat it. Then she realized that the pot was still bubbling away and it was getting fuller and fuller. She wanted to stop it, but she couldn't remember how!

"That's enough!" she cried, but the pot bubbled and boiled, and porridge started to trickle over the edges.

"Don't cook, little pot!" she begged, but the porridge poured over the table and dripped onto the floor.

"Stop cooking now, please!" wailed the mother. But, by now, the porridge was flowing out of the magic pot and all over the cottage.

Before long, the porridge was spilling out through the door and gushing down the lane that led to the village.

"Please, little pot, no more!" howled the mother, but it was no good—she was too panic-stricken to remember how to make the porridge pot stop.

She waded out of the cottage to look for her daughter, but all she could see was porridge! It had oozed down the lane, across the fields, and into all the houses in the village.

The villagers were standing outside, up to their knees in porridge, holding their pets and farm animals in their arms to save them. There was enough porridge to feed ten villages!

Just then, the little girl stepped out of the forest and was surprised to see a tide of porridge heading straight for her. She waded home as quickly as

she could, though the porridge came up to her waist. When she reached her cottage, she fought her way past her mother, through the door, and cried out, "Stop, little pot, stop!"

At last, the magic pot came to a halt and the porridge stopped pouring out. Her mother sighed with relief and everyone in the village cheered.

That day, the little girl and her mother threw a big porridge party and invited everyone who lived in the villages around them to bring a bowl and spoon to help clean up. Even the pets and farm animals helped to eat it up!

When all the porridge was gone, they placed the magic porridge pot in the middle of the village square with instructions on how to use it. That way, the pot never overflowed again and nobody—friend or stranger—ever went hungry again.

The Proud Peacock

At the dawn of time, all the animals in the world got together to decide who would rule over them. The animals of the land chose the lion, the animals of the sea chose the whale, and the animals of the sky chose the swan.

In time, the swan king had a beautiful daughter with feathers even more bright and gleaming than his own. When she was young, the king granted her one wish. The swan princess wished that, one day, she could choose her own husband.

When she was old enough, the swan king summoned all the birds so that the swan princess could find a husband who was good enough to marry her.

Birds flew from far and wide to meet the swan princess, and soon the lake was alive with their noisy chirps and twitters. There were black swans and white swans, geese and ducks, eagles and owls, sparrows and starlings, blackbirds and bluebirds, kingfishers and hummingbirds, parrots, macaws, lovebirds, and more!

"Now, my daughter, you may choose who you wish to marry," said her father.

There were so many beautiful birds, it took the swan princess a whole day to meet them all. Many of the birds were incredibly handsome, but one bird caught her eye—it was a magnificent peacock with a long elegant neck, an amazing fan of emerald and cobalt blue feathers, and a delicate crown upon its head. She thought the two of them would surely make a fine match!

She glided over to the king and said, "I choose the peacock for my husband, Father." And the swan king made his announcement: "With so much beauty here, it was a difficult decision, but the princess has chosen the peacock for her husband. Let us sing his praise."

The birds sang in celebration and congratulated the peacock. "Lucky you!" they tweeted, and many of the birds bowed before him and brought him gifts.

All the attention quickly went to the peacock's head and he proudly puffed up his chest, fanned out his feathers, stretched his long neck, and pointed his beak to the heavens. Then, he began to perform a strange dance. He hopped from side to side, strutted around in a circle, let out a long squawk, and then—forgetting that he was in the presence of royalty—he bent over to show off his splendid tail feathers, wiggling his bottom from side to side at the swan king and princess!

The flock gasped with shock and some of the younger birds giggled—the proud peacock had got so carried away, he had made a complete fool of himself.

The swan king was unhappy to see the peacock behaving with such bad manners. "Peacock!" he cried. "Your pride in winning the princess's heart has made you behave like a shameless show-off—and I won't let my daughter marry someone who makes a fool of himself in public. You will not be her prince!"

The peacock was so embarrassed, he flew away as quickly as he could, in a flap and flurry of feathers. And that is where the saying,

"pride comes before a fall"

comes from!

The Monkey and the Crocodile

A tribe of noisy monkeys lived together in a great tree by a river where the crocodiles basked and hunted.

Every day, the monkeys would tiptoe down to the water to take a sip, and, every day, the crocodiles would lie in wait and try to snap them up in their mighty jaws —but the monkeys were always too quick. One day, the smartest and bravest of the monkeys was admiring an island in the middle of the river, which was covered in fruit trees. "Wouldn't it be good to dine on those sweet fruits?" he asked his family.

They all agreed. "But it's too far to jump. It's dangerous! Those greedy crocodiles will snap you up!" wailed the monkey's mother.

The monkey studied the river and spotted a large flat rock jutting out of the water, halfway between the riverbank and the island.

"I think I could make it across if I hop onto that rock," said the clever little monkey. "And then we can all have a big feast to celebrate!"

And so it was decided. The brave monkey ran to the edge of the river, leapt onto the rock, and then made it in a single bound onto the island.

Once there, he saw many different types of luscious fruit hanging from the trees. He ate lots of them and the sweet, sticky juice dribbled down his chin, then he grabbed as many as he could and jumped onto the rock again.

▲⋮//////▲⋮//////▲⋮//////▲⋮

As he leapt from the rock to the bank of the river, one of the big, greedy crocodiles saw him.

"Ha!" thought the crocodile. "Do that again and I'll catch you in my jaws and gobble you up!"

So the big crocodile swam to where the monkey was making his leap over the river and snapped at the monkey's tail as he jumped.

But each time the monkey leapt from the riverbank to the rock to the island and back again, he was just too quick and too high for the crocodile. After a whole day of snapping, the crocodile was in a very bad mood.

One of the smaller crocodiles, who had been watching, said, "I know how you can catch that monkey. If I tell you, will you share your feast?"

"Sure," said the big crocodile—but, really, he had no intention of sharing. He was far too greedy for that.

"Your skin looks a lot like that rock. Why don't you just drape yourself over it and when the monkey leaps onto you, you can grab him?"

The big crocodile thought this was an excellent idea. The next morning, he draped himself over the rock, with his head facing the island, so the monkey wouldn't see him—and he waited.

▲·/////▲·/////▲·/////▲

Now, the monkeys had enjoyed their feast of fruit so much, they begged

their clever monkey friend to jump over to the island and grab some more treats to eat. But when he reached the riverbank that morning, the rock didn't look right. It seemed to have grown overnight.

"Hmmm," thought the little monkey. "Something funny is going on here."

He looked up and down the river for the big crocodile who had snapped at him, but he was nowhere to be seen.

"Is that rock scaly now or is my mind playing tricks? I think I will check."

"Oh, good morning, rock!" cried the monkey. "How are you today? You seem to have grown bigger, or are my eyes deceiving me?"

The crocodile wasn't sure what to do, so he stayed quiet.

"Hey, rock! Are you unwell? Why haven't you greeted me like you always do? Why are you so quiet?"

The silly crocodile thought that he must be lying on a talking rock, so he spoke up.

The Monkey and the Crocodile

"Oh, good morning, monkey!" he said. "I didn't see you there."

The monkey laughed. "Ha! So it is you, crocodile! Waiting to catch me, were you? Well, I'll make a deal with you—you can eat me for your lunch, if you let me jump onto the island and have one last fruity feast first."

The crocodile thought it sounded fair enough, so he agreed. The monkey leapt onto his back, then onto the island to pick the low-hanging fruit.

"Now I have him trapped," grinned the crocodile, and he grew impatient, thinking about the wonderful lunch he was about to enjoy.

When the monkey had finally finished eating, he loaded his arms with fruit.

"Hey! What's that for?" asked the hungry crocodile. "I don't want fruit!"

"Perhaps you could grant one last wish for me, crocodile?" asked the monkey. "Let me deliver this fruit to my family on the other side of the river. Then I promise I will jump into your mouth!"

"Deal," said the crocodile. And the monkey leapt onto his head, onto the riverbank, then ran straight up a tree.

"Hey, come back!" said the foolish crocodile. "You made a deal!"

"Yes!" shouted the monkey, as he handed the fruit to his family. "And only a fool would have believed it!"

And that is how the crocodile learned that if something sounds too good to be true, it probably is!

The Children of Lir

Long ago, in a time of magic and fairies, Ireland was ruled over by a great king called Lir, who had four beautiful children—happy Fionnula, bold Aodh, and beautiful twin brothers, Fiacra and Conn.

Everyone in Ireland adored King Lir's children—even the fairies, who gave them each a gift of a snowy white horse, swifter than the wind. All was well with the royal family until the queen died of a sudden and unexpected illness. The children were still young and King Lir felt they needed a mother to care for them, so he found a new wife as quickly as he could. This new queen—Aoife—was full of charm with King Lir, but when she saw how the king doted on his children, and how the fairies loved them, and how the people of Ireland adored them, her heart grew black with jealousy and hatred.

Aoife was really a witch and, as her dislike for the children grew, she began to look for spells to get rid of them, so that she could finally be alone with King Lir.

One day, she drove the children in her chariot to a nearby lake to teach them how to swim. As soon as the children began bathing, she waded out to them and struck them with her wand. As she did so, she muttered a curse under her breath. One by one, each child was transformed into an elegant snow-white swan.

The children panicked, stretching their long necks and flapping their wings in distress.

"Be calm," smiled Queen Aoife. "It's not so bad—I could have done a lot worse. Children, you are now cursed to swim on this lake for 300 years, and on the Irish Sea for another 300 years, and on the waters around the Isle of Inishglora for another 300 years. After this, only the ring of a church bell will save you."

Fionnula shouted angrily and was surprised to find that she still had her voice, "How you could do this, you wicked woman? When our father finds

out what has happened, a more terrible fate than ours will greet you!"

But, relieved at last to be rid of the children, Queen Aoife just laughed. She escaped in her chariot and the four children tried to follow her, but no matter how hard they flapped their wings, they could not fly beyond the shores of the lake. That night, the sight of four swans weeping as the sun set over the mountains was the saddest thing Ireland had ever seen.

There was much sadness in the castle of King Lir too, when his wicked wife told him that his four precious children had been killed by wild boars. All of Ireland grieved for their lost princess and princes, but none suffered more than the king. One day, he rode out to the lake to grieve in peace when four swans suddenly landed at his feet.

"Father! It is us—your children!" cried the largest swan.

King Lir could not believe what he was hearing—the swan sounded exactly like his beloved daughter, Fionnula. He thought he must have gone mad with grief, but his swan children quickly explained what had happened.

He embraced them sadly and promised to visit them every day, then he returned to his castle, where he banished his cruel wife from Ireland forever.

From that day, King Lir made sure that the lake of his swan children was always protected and he made it a law that no swan could ever be harmed or killed in Ireland. He visited his children every day and, when news spread of what had happened, the lake attracted hundreds of visitors. The royal swans entertained everyone with their beautiful singing and, for many years, they lived happily.

But, in time, their father passed away and the children of Lir faded from people's memories, until their fate became nothing but a long-forgotten story—a whisper from the past. After 300 years on the lake, the swan children flew to the Irish Sea, where they spent another 300 years on the crashing, stormy waves.

Finally, their curse took them to the uninhabited Isle of Inishglora, where fishermen told stories of the mysterious white swans they had heard singing sweetly across the waters.

At last, their 900-year curse came to an end. The four swan children flew back to the home of their childhood, only to find it in ruins. As they landed, they heard a church bell ringing, and as their feet touched the ground, their feathers fell away and the four magnificent singing swans—Fionnula, Aodh, Fiacra, and Conn—transformed into children once again. Nobody knew what to make of the incredible story told by the children of Lir, but they told it so often that it has never been forgotten—and it will live on for many years to come.

The Little Fir Tree

In the heart of the forest, there stood a young fir tree. It grew in a fine spot with plenty of fresh air and sunlight, but it was surrounded by trees that were far taller and stronger than itself.

The little fir tree would look up at the other trees and wish that it was big and strong too. In its first winter, a hare hopped right over the little fir tree. It shook its branches with irritation and was so cross that it barely noticed the beauty of the snowy forest around it.

"We know! We know!" said two fat robins

"Where are they going? Will they get to see the world?" wondered the little fir tree.

"We know! We know!" said two fat robins. "We flew into town and we peeped through the windows. Such magnificence awaits them! They will be planted in pots in warm rooms, and decorated with gingerbread, and pretty toys, and candles!"

Every twig of the fir tree trembled at the thought of it. "Oh, how I wish I could live in someone's room and be decorated with beautiful things!"

"Oh, little fir tree," sparkled the sunbeams. "Rejoice in your youth!"

"Oh, little fir tree," sang the birds. "Stay and enjoy the green forest!"

"Oh, little fir tree," whispered the wind. "Let me play in your branches."

When spring came, it didn't notice the children who had their picnics by its side; the baby birds that played among its branches; or the sunbeams that danced among its needles. All the little fir tree could think was, "I wish I would grow up quickly. I wish I could see what the world is like."

One year passed and then another, and though the little fir tree grew, it was never quite fast enough. "Why can't I grow more quickly?" it sighed.

One snowy winter, some woodcutters came by and chopped down some of the taller, more handsome trees in the green forest.

But the little fir tree didn't listen and every day it longed to be somewhere else—somewhere more exciting.

Over the next year, it grew into a tall, strong tree. Everyone who passed by said how beautiful it was. When the woodcutters returned in winter, it was the first tree to be cut down.

"At last!" thought the fir tree. It was placed in a horse-drawn cart and carried to a large house. Two servants lifted the fir tree into the house and set it down in a grand drawing room.

The room was filled with fine paintings, furniture, and ornate vases. There were velvet curtains and silken sofas, and a beautiful window, where a pot stood waiting for the tree.

The fir tree shivered with excitement as it was placed in the pot. "What will happen next?" it wondered.

Several servants came into the room and sighed at the sight of the lovely fir tree. They started to hang beautiful decorations all over its branches— there were small net bags filled with sweets, golden apples and clusters of walnuts, miniature dolls, wooden toys, bright shining baubles, and hundreds of tiny candles, stuck to the branches with melted wax. Finally, at the very top of the tree, they placed a shimmering gold star.

"How the tree will shine tonight!" said the servants.

"Oh, if only tonight would come!" thought the impatient fir tree. "And then what? Will I stay here forever, dressed like this?" It longed so badly for the evening to come quickly.

Later that night, a servant came to light every candle, so that the fir tree looked dazzlingly beautiful. A family dressed in fine clothing came into the room, and the children gasped with delight to see the magnificence of the fir tree.

The tree's branches quivered with uncertainty. "What will they do to me now? Will I stay here?" it worried.

Soon the family were singing carols around the tree, and the little ones danced around it, ruffling its branches as they went. Later, a maid came to snuff out the candles and the children began plundering the fir tree for its hidden toys and treats. Nobody paid any attention to the tree now—they were too busy playing with their gifts.

At last, the children tugged on the sleeve of one of the older men. "Daddy, tell us a story!" they begged. He smiled and sat down next to the tree, where he told them the story of Humpty Dumpty, who fell off a wall, but married a princess and became a king. It was a wonderful story—the first the tree had ever heard.

"Maybe that will happen to me," the tree thought. "One day, I might fall over and marry a princess too. Perhaps I will become a king?"

When the stories were over, the fir tree was left alone in the room and it thought, "I will try not to tremble or worry tomorrow. I will be still and straight, so I can enjoy it more and the children can admire me better."

However, when the morning came, none of the children returned. Instead, two servants dug the fir tree out of its pot, and carried it up to a dark, dusty corner of the attic.

The fir tree lay alone in the darkness for many hours, wondering what might happen next in its adventures.

"It's winter outside now," thought the tree. "Perhaps that is why I am here—the ground is too cold and hard to plant me again. They must be waiting for spring to come round again!"

And so the fir tree lay patiently in the dark, dusty attic for many long days and nights, and it often thought, "How nice it would be to feel the sunbeams or the breeze on my branches right now. How I miss the hare that used to hop over me, and the beauty of the forest I grew up in!"

One night, two little mice appeared at the fir tree's side, squeaking and rustling among its branches.

"It might be nice and warm here in the branches of this old tree," said one mouse to the other.

"I'm not an old tree!" said the fir tree. "There are many trees older than me in the forest!"

"Oh, do tell us where you came from!" said the mice, excited to have some company. "Have you seen the world? We have only ever seen inside the food cupboard."

So the fir tree told them of the world it had seen—the green forest with the singing birds, the shimmering snow in winter, the pretty flowers in summer. It told them of the hare that used to hop over it, and the sunbeams and the wild wind that played amongst its branches. It told them of its journey to the house and how its branches had been so beautifully decorated. It told them of the singing, dancing children, and the story of Humpty Dumpty.

"How lucky you have been!" gasped the mice. "How happy you must have been!" they squeaked.

And, all of a sudden, the fir tree felt quite foolish for not realizing it at the time. "Yes, and how silly I have been," said the tree quietly, and it sat in the dark, wishing for its old life again.

One fine day at the end of winter, two servants came into the attic and carried the fir tree out into the bright daylight. They left it in a wild corner of the garden, next to the weeds and the grass cuttings, but the fir tree didn't mind at all—the sun shone brightly and, once more, the sunbeams danced on its yellowing branches. The cool breeze ruffled what was left of its needles and a fat robin landed on a branch, near to its only remaining Christmas decoration—the golden star at the top. As the tree looked around at the spring blossoms and the blue sky, it suddenly realized how very lucky its life had been.

The Greedy Fox

It was a cold harsh winter and the animals of the forest were very hungry—especially Fox, who hadn't eaten a scrap of food for days.

"It's okay for Bear," shivered Fox, feeling sorry for himself. "She gets to curl up for the winter in her cosy cave with a full belly, dreaming of warmer days."

"And Squirrel can't complain!" he moaned. "He's been burying his secret fruit and nut supplies all over the place for months. But a fox? A fox like me has to hunt for food whatever the weather!"

Fox shook the freshly fallen snow from his coat and slumped to the ground. His tummy ached with hunger, but he felt so tired and weak, he soon fell asleep.

He was woken later that morning by the loud crunch, crunch of someone walking on snow. He opened his eyes to see a woodcutter pushing a large package into the hollow of a nearby tree. The woodcutter, who was bundled up in thick, warm clothes, seemed very pleased with his hiding place. He whistled happily to himself and went on his way—he didn't see Fox lying close by, covered in a thick layer of snow.

Fox sniffed the air, hopefully. "I must be dreaming!" he thought. "Is that chicken I can smell? Is hunger making me imagine things?"

But an icy breeze wafted past Fox and there it was again—the unmistakable aroma of roast chicken, coming from the tree hollow. It was impossible to resist.

Fox used all his energy to walk over to the tree and, inside its thin hollow, he spied the package. One sniff told him that this was no dream—it really was filled with delicious food.

"How can I get to it?" thought Fox desperately. "I'll never fit inside such a long, thin space."

But Fox was so terribly hungry, he knew he had to try. He pushed his head and shoulders as far into the hollow as he could, then tried to squeeze in his body. Much to his surprise, he had become so thin, he could fit inside quite easily.

Once inside the hollow, he quickly tore open the woodcutter's bag and his eyes lit up at the feast before him.

There was enough food to feed a fox for many days. There were two roast chickens, a side of baked ham, a loaf of bread and several rolls, huge hunks of cheese, and three big rosy apples.

Fox couldn't believe his good fortune and, within minutes, he had gobbled up a whole chicken. It was delicious—the best thing he had ever tasted! However, as he hadn't eaten for so long, his tummy quickly felt full.

"But I can't leave all this food here," thought Fox. "What if another animal finds it? Or what if the woodcutter takes it away again? What if I don't find any more food this winter?"

So, despite his bulging belly, Fox carried on eating. He ate the second chicken, the baked ham, the loaf of bread, the hunks of cheese, and all three apples. By the time he had finished, Fox had more than satisfied his hunger and his tummy felt quite fit to burst.

"I should get out of here," he sighed. "I don't want to get caught by that woodcutter with his axe."

So Fox heaved himself up and tried to squeeze out of the hollow. But, this time, he wasn't quite so thin. In fact, his tummy was now so big and round,

he couldn't get out at all. Try as he might, he was trapped inside the tree!

Luckily for him, while he had been scoffing all the food, the snow had fallen so heavily that the woodcutter couldn't find his way back to the tree.

Greedy Fox was forced to stay in the hollow for many days until he was thin enough to squeeze his way out again. As he leapt onto the snowy forest floor, he promised himself that he would never be so foolish and greedy again.

The Mermaid of Zennor

In the small fishing village of Zennor, on the rugged coast of north Cornwall, stands a church that is over 1,400 years old.

For many years, all the villagers, including the fishermen, gathered in this church every Sunday to give thanks and pray for a good catch the following week. Every service would end with beautiful hymns from the choir and the whole village would join them in song.

Every so often, a mysterious cloaked woman would quietly slip through the door of the church and stand in the shadows at the back, listening to the choir with a contented smile on her face. She always slipped away again before the hymns ended so that no one could see her.

One summer evening, a new member joined the choir—a young fisherman named Matthew Trewella. Not only was Matthew the most handsome man for many a mile, he also sang like an angel. That night, his silvery voice carried on the breeze down to the small cove, where the fishing boats bobbed, the seagulls soared, and a mermaid sat on a rock, combing her hair and looking at the church with great joy.

The mermaid's name was Morveren and, though she loved her life in the watery depths, she enjoyed nothing more than hearing the songs of the men and women of Zennor. She looked forward to it every week and, on rare occasions, when her father allowed it, she even sneaked into the church to hear it better. Morveren was the mysterious woman in the cloak.

On this night, when she heard the voice of Matthew Trewella, she thought it was more beautiful than any she had ever heard before. She longed to be near it.

The following week, Morveren begged her father—the king of the sea—to allow her to visit Zennor again. Though he disapproved of his daughter's visits, he saw how much they meant to her, so he allowed her to go, on the condition that this would be the last time.

Morveren combed her long hair and dressed in a pearl-encrusted floor-length gown to disguise her mermaid tail. She draped a sea-green cloak about her shoulders and sat on the rock, waiting for the wonderful singing to begin.

Soon enough, she heard Matthew Trewella's magnificent voice carrying on the breeze and she stepped out of the sea, following the magical music all the way to the church. As always, Morveren crept in quietly and lingered in the shadows, hoping that nobody would see her. But when she saw Matthew singing, she couldn't help but step forward into the light. She even pulled down the hood of her cloak, so that she could see his handsome face and hear his beautiful song more clearly.

He was completely enchanted by her beauty...

Just as she did so, Matthew Trewella looked up to see Morveren and was unable to take his eyes away from her—he was completely enchanted by her beauty. Morveren smiled at him and he sang more brightly and brilliantly than he had ever sung before. The village was filled with the sound of his angelic voice.

When the end of the service came, Morveren slipped away, as always, but Matthew Trewella—determined not to lose sight of her—abandoned the choir, ran down the church aisle and followed her out of the door.

The Mermaid of Zennor

And that was the last the people of Zennor saw of handsome Matthew Trewella. His disappearance was a great mystery, until several years later when a local fisherman dropped his anchor out at sea, just beyond the cove.

A beautiful mermaid appeared alongside the ship and hailed the captain. She asked him if he would kindly move his anchor, as it was blocking her front door and she needed to get home to her children and her husband, Matthew.

The captain agreed and pulled up his anchor. When he returned to the village of Zennor later that day, he wrote in the parish records that Matthew Trewella had been lured out to sea by a mermaid.

For many years, local fishermen claimed that they could hear Matthew singing to his mermaid wife every night as the sun set over the sea. Some people say they can still hear him.

The Twelve Dancing Princesses

Once upon a time, there was a king who had twelve daughters. These princesses loved each other very much and spent all their time together—they even shared a bedroom.

But they had a secret that drove the king mad with curiosity—every night when they went to bed, their door was locked, but by the morning, their shoes were so worn out they had big holes in the soles. It was as though they had danced all night.

One morning, when the maid presented the king with twelve more tattered pairs of shoes, he summoned his daughters to the throne room.

"Look at the state of these shoes! Do you have any idea how much money I spend on new pairs? Tell me, once and for all, what do you do all night? Where do you go?"

The eldest princess smiled and said innocently, "We don't know what you mean, Papa!"

The king sighed. "Very well, then. If you won't tell me the truth, I'll just have to find out for myself!"

That day, the king issued an important announcement saying that whoever could find out how the princesses wore out their shoes every night would be given a knighthood.

The news spread quickly and, soon, a prince presented himself at the palace. The king was impressed by the prince's manners and tales of

heroism, and led him to a chamber by the princesses' bedroom. He told the prince to watch the princesses to see how they wore out their shoes.

As the king's footsteps faded away, the princesses came to chat to the prince and offered him a cup of hot cocoa with a sleeping potion in it. Within moments, the prince fell into a deep sleep. When he woke the next day, the princesses were sound asleep in their beds, but their new shoes were in tatters. The prince had failed and the king was disappointed.

After that, many more brave knights and princes tried their luck, but all were tricked by the sleeping potion— and the king was getting annoyed.

One day, a young soldier came to the city. He was making his way to the palace when he met an old woman.

"Where are you heading, young man?"

"I'm going to the castle to discover the mystery of the twelve princesses—I thought I'd try my luck."

"You seem like an honest fellow," said the woman, "so I'll tell you something and I'll give you something.

"I tell you to pour away the cocoa the princesses offer to you tonight, and I give you this invisibility cloak. Wear it when you follow them."

The soldier thanked the wise woman for her advice and he headed to the castle, filled with confidence.

By now, the king had grown weary of meeting dashing young men, so he didn't have much hope when he saw the soldier. However, he led him to the chamber and wished him luck.

The soldier found the princesses to be friendly and charming and, when the eldest princess offered him some cocoa, he accepted. But when no one was looking, he poured it away.

The princesses went to bed and waited until they heard him snoring. "Poor thing," said the youngest of the twelve. "I like him."

"Do you like him enough to miss our fun?" asked the eldest princess.

The younger sister sighed. "I have a strange feeling about tonight."

"You'll forget all about it when we're there," laughed her sister.

And the princesses got out of bed, changed into their finest ball gowns and slipped on their new shoes.

When they were ready, the eldest princess knocked three times on the headboard of her bed. Instantly, it slid to one side to reveal a secret trapdoor. The soldier opened his eyes just in time to see the princesses disappear down some dark steps.

As quiet as a mouse, he draped the cloak of invisibility around himself and followed them down the flight of stairs and along a tunnel carved out of rock. As they walked along, the soldier accidentally stepped on the hem of the youngest princess's dress.

"Wait!" cried the princess. "Somebody grabbed my dress!"

"Don't be silly!" said her sisters. "You must have caught it on something."

Soon the tunnel gave way to a path that led through an enchanted wood.

In the first glade, the leaves were made from shining silver, which

glistened in the moonlight. The soldier snapped off a twig and the youngest princess jumped with fright.

"What was that?" said the princess.

Then they came to a glade where the leaves were made of pure gold. The soldier snapped off another twig.

Next, they came to a glade where the leaves were made of pure, sparkling diamonds. Again, the soldier snapped off a twig and the youngest princess cried out, "Something isn't right!"

Soon they reached a lake where twelve boats awaited them. In each boat, there sat a handsome prince.

Each princess stepped into her own boat, and the soldier quietly crept in and sat behind the youngest princess. The prince, who was rowing, huffed and puffed and said, "Excuse me, but the boat seems harder to row tonight."

At last they reached the other side of the lake—and there the soldier saw a splendid castle. It was all lit up and alive with the sound of music.

As they stepped inside, the soldier was astonished to see a spectacular ballroom, with an orchestra playing music so wonderful that it instantly made him want to dance.

At once, the princesses began to dance with

their princes, waltzing and twirling around!

At four o'clock in the morning, the music ended and the princes escorted the princesses back to the lake and rowed them to the enchanted wood.

Still wrapped in his invisibility cloak, the soldier crept into the youngest sister's boat and saw that her shoes were completely worn through.

When they reached the shore, the soldier dashed back to the castle. By the time the princesses returned, he was lying in bed, pretending to snore.

The princesses changed out of their ball gowns and placed their tattered shoes by their beds. "See," yawned the eldest princess. "Nothing to fear."

The next morning, the time came for the soldier to report to the king, and the princesses were summoned too.

"So what do my daughters do every night?" asked the king.

"They go dancing in the ballroom of a secret castle!" said the soldier.

The youngest sister gasped, but the eldest stood up and said, "Prove it!"

The soldier told the king the whole story—of the secret trapdoor, the hidden tunnel, the enchanted wood, the lake, the boats, the twelve princes, and the splendid castle!

Then he handed the king a twig with silver leaves, a twig of gold, and a twig of diamonds. It was no use, the twelve dancing princesses had to confess.

The king was cross, but not for long —when he saw how much his twelve daughters loved to dance, he agreed to host a ball every month. Meanwhile, the soldier became a knight—and, in time, he married the youngest princess, who taught him how to dance!

The Snow Child

On the edge of a forest in Russia, lived a couple called Sergei and Maria. Though they had lived long and healthy lives, they had never felt truly happy, because they had always longed for a child.

They loved to watch the local children play, but it wasn't quite the same as having a child of their very own.

One winter, the snow fell deep in the forest—deeper than ever before. When it finally stopped, the village children squealed with delight as they jumped into snowdrifts and threw snowballs at each other. Sergei and Maria watched them fondly.

When the children started to build snowmen, Sergei laughed and said, "Let's join them! Let's make our own snowman!"

"Why not?" chuckled Maria. They wrapped themselves up warmly and went out into the sparkling snow.

As they started to build, Maria said, "Anyone can make a snowman. Let's make our own little snow child instead!"

And so the two set to work building and shaping the body, giving it two little arms and two little legs. Next, they started on the head. The village children soon gathered round.

"What are you making?" they asked.

"A snow child!" laughed the couple.

They gave their snow child curly hair, a sweet little nose, cute dimpled cheeks, and two blue beads for eyes. Finally, Sergei carved out the mouth.

The couple stepped back to admire their work and, just as they did so, the snow child let out a warm breath and smiled. The icy snow magically melted away from its face and there, before them, was a little girl with eyes as blue as forget-me-nots, lips as red as cherries, a tangle of blonde ringlets, and snow-white skin.

"Am I dreaming?" said Sergei, rubbing his eyes, but Maria didn't hear him —she had already run to the little girl and had thrown her arms around her. The girl hugged Maria tightly.

"It's a miracle!" cried Maria. "Our wish has been granted at last! Come, little Snegurochka," as she named the snow child, "we must get you warm."

And Maria led the little girl into their cottage, leaving Sergei and the rest of the village children lost for words.

Little Snegurochka was indeed a miracle and every day Sergei and Maria's cottage was filled with visitors, eager to meet the famous snow child. Snegurochka quickly made friends with the village children and they played together all winter, filling the village with the sound of joy and laughter. Sergei and Maria had never been happier.

At last, winter drew to a close and the snow melted away. The spring sun warmed the earth and, soon, the first flowers began to blossom. Birds sang cheerfully and all felt bright and gay —all except for Snegurochka, who grew sadder with each passing day.

As it grew warmer outside, the snow child stopped going out to play and, instead, spent her days curled up in dark corners of the cottage or in the shadow of a tree. But when the sun went down, Snegurochka returned to her joyful, playful self.

Sergei and Maria started to worry for their little girl, so when the village children invited Snegurochka to a forest picnic, they thought it was a good idea—the trees would protect her from the sun she so disliked and she would be sure to have some fun.

Snegurochka wanted to stay at home, but the couple urged her to go. "It will do you some good to play with your friends, dear!" they smiled.

Before she left, Maria said to the children, "Please take care of our little Snegurochka!"

And, as they skipped into the trees, the village children called, "Don't worry, Maria, we will!"

Snegurochka did have fun that day. With her playmates, she made pretty crowns from wild flowers, and fairy wands from twigs.

They built dens and played hide and seek, and when the sun sank in the sky, some of the older children made a fire and they gathered around it to sing merry songs and tell stories. As the fire started to dwindle, the children began to play a new game. They all arranged themselves in a long line and, one after another, jumped over the glowing embers and made a wish.

"Just do as we do, Snegurochka!" they explained.

But when it came to Snegurochka's turn, the children heard a loud sigh and when they turned round to see her jump over the fire, she had gone.

"Where can she be?" they wondered.

"She must be hiding from us!" said one of the girls, and the children ran into the trees to look for Snegurochka, but they couldn't find her anywhere.

"Perhaps she went home?" said a boy, so they set off for her cottage. But when they found that she wasn't there and told Sergei and Maria what had happened, everyone's happiness soon turned to sadness and worry.

For many days after that, Sergei and Maria and all the adults in the village hunted high and low for Snegurochka, but she was nowhere to be seen.

At last, the couple found themselves back at the spot where the children had made their bonfire.

In the ashes, Sergei saw something twinkling in the light and, when he looked closely, he found a solid silver snowflake, no bigger than a charm you'd find on a necklace.

All at once, he and Maria guessed what had happened—their precious little girl of snow had leapt over the flames of the fire and its heat had melted her away. The silver snowflake was all that remained of her.

For the rest of her days, Maria wore the silver snowflake around her neck so that she could always remember the magical winter they had enjoyed with their beloved little Snegurochka —the snow child.

East of the Sun and West of the Moon

There was once a poor peasant who had many children and little money to feed them. He loved all his children, but his eldest daughter, Astrid, was the most clever and good-hearted of them all.

One stormy night, the peasant and his children were huddled by the fire, when there was a knock at the door.

The peasant opened the door to discover a magnificent white bear towering above him.

"Good evening, sir," said the White Bear in a deep and rumbling voice.

"I have come to ask for the company of your eldest daughter. If she agrees to stay with me for just one year, I will not harm her and I promise that I will return and make you very rich."

Though he loved his daughter very much, the peasant didn't enjoy being poor and hungry, so he went to talk to Astrid. Of course, she said no at first, but deep down she knew it was best for her family so, with a heavy heart, she agreed to go with the bear.

Astrid smartened up her rags and met the White Bear politely. He asked her to climb on his back and she sadly waved goodbye to her family.

Astrid clung tightly to the bear's fur and they rode far away until they reached a great mountain. The White Bear thudded on the side of the mountain with his giant paw and a large door opened up in the rock.

The entrance led to a glorious castle with brilliantly lit rooms, all decorated with gleaming gold and silver, and a banqueting hall, filled with fine foods.

The White Bear was kind to Astrid. He gave her a silver bell and told her that all she had to do was ring it and anything she wished for would appear.

Astrid clung tightly to the bear's fur and they rode away until they reached a great mountain

When the time came for bed, Astrid sleepily rang the silver bell and a beautiful bedchamber magically appeared with a luxurious bed, draped in sheets made of pure silk.

She lay down wearily and put out the light, but in the middle of the night, someone came into the room and lay down beside her. She could just make out his outline in the darkness and it wasn't a bear—it was a man. But, when she awoke the next morning, the mysterious stranger had gone.

Over the next few weeks, Astrid saw little of the White Bear but, every night, the stranger came to her chamber and lay down beside her, then disappeared before dawn. Astrid grew more and more curious.

One night, she used her magic bell to wish for a candle. She hid it under her pillow and, when she was sure that the man was fast asleep, she lit it. She was amazed to see a young man lying there. He had such a kind face that she fell in love with him straight away. In her surprise, Astrid spilled candle wax on his shirt and woke him.

She was amazed to see a young man lying there

"Oh no!" he cried. "My wicked stepmother, the Queen, put a curse on me, which makes me a white bear by day and a man by night. It could only be broken if I spent a year in the company of someone good-hearted, like you. Now she will force me to marry the troll princess!"

Astrid wept guilty tears. "Please try to save me," begged the Prince. "You must journey to the castle that is east of the sun and west of the moon." And, with that, the Prince vanished, along with the castle and the silver bell.

Astrid found herself lying on the forest floor, dressed in rags again. Deeply sorry, she set out to find the Prince.

She walked for many long days until she came to the edge of the forest, where a wise old woman sat with a golden apple in her hands.

Astrid asked the old woman if she knew the way to the Prince who lived in the castle that was east of the sun and west of the moon.

"I know nothing of it," said the woman, "but you can ride my white horse to my friend, who may know more. Here, take this golden apple for good luck."

So Astrid rode the white horse to a second wise old woman who sat outside a tumbledown cottage with a golden comb in her hands.

Astrid asked if she knew the way to the Prince who lived in the castle that was east of the sun and west of the moon.

"I know nothing of it," she said kindly, "but you can ride my black horse to my friend, who may know more. Take this golden comb for good luck."

So Astrid mounted the black horse and rode to a third old woman, who sat by a golden spinning wheel.

Astrid asked the third old woman if she knew the way to the Prince who lived in the castle that was east of the sun and west of the moon.

"I know nothing of it," said the woman, "but you can ride my silver horse to the North Wind, who knows more. Take this golden spinning wheel for luck."

Astrid rode for many more days until, at last, she reached the North Wind. Exhausted, she asked the North Wind

if he knew the way to the Prince who lived in the castle that was east of the sun and west of the moon.

"I know the way," said the North Wind. "I blew a leaf there once. If you are not afraid, I can blow you there, too."

The North Wind puffed himself up and blew as hard as he could. Astrid was sent rushing through the air, over the mountains and across the sea until she reached the castle that was east of the sun and west of the moon.

Astrid was standing near the castle with the golden apple in her hands, when a bossy voice called out. "You there! How much do you want for that golden apple?" Astrid looked up to see a lady with cold, mean eyes and a piggy nose—it was the troll princess!

Astrid answered cleverly. "It can't be bought for money, but if you let me be with the Prince tonight, it is yours."

The troll princess agreed to the deal with a sly smile but, when Astrid was finally allowed into the Prince's chamber that night, he was fast asleep and nothing could stir him. The scheming troll princess had put sleeping potion in his cocoa! Astrid sobbed with frustration until the guards came to take her away again.

Later that day, outside the castle, Astrid sat combing her hair with the golden comb. The troll princess saw it from her window. She was spoilt and wanted the comb very much.

"You again!" she shouted. "How much do you want for that golden comb?"

Astrid answered as before. "It can't be bought for money, but if you let me be with the Prince tonight, it is yours."

So Astrid was allowed into the castle and, again, she found that the troll princess had tricked her—the Prince

Astrid was sent rushing through the air, over the mountains and across the sea...

was in an unbreakable slumber. Astrid wept until the guards came to take her away again in the morning.

Later that day, Astrid sat outside the castle walls, this time spinning on her golden spinning wheel. The troll princess saw it and, of course, she demanded it. Astrid gave the same answer as before.

"It can't be bought for money," she said, "but if you let me be with the Prince tonight, it is yours."

Now it so happened that one of the guards liked the Prince and had heard Astrid crying in the Prince's chamber. He took pity on her and told the Prince what had been happening. That evening, when the troll princess offered to make a mug of cocoa for the Prince, he accepted, but secretly poured it away.

When Astrid entered his chamber that night, the Prince was overjoyed to see her, but he told her that the Queen was forcing him to marry the troll princess the next day. Before the guards came to take Astrid away, the pair came up with a clever plan.

On the morning of the wedding, the Prince asked the Queen if he could set a small test for his bride-to-be. "I suppose so," she sighed reluctantly.

"I have a fine shirt that I wish to wear for my wedding," said the Prince, "but it has some candle wax on it. I will only marry the woman who can wash it off."

The troll princess scoffed at such a silly task and began to wash the shirt but, as she did so, the wax spots grew bigger. With each scrub, they spread until the shirt was dirty all over.

"Why, you can't even do a simple thing like that!" said the Prince. "There is a girl in rags outside the castle—I bet she can do better. Bring her in, guards!"

The guards summoned Astrid and the Prince set her the same challenge. As soon as she dipped the dirty shirt, it looked whiter than freshly fallen snow.

Astrid and the Prince were delighted that their plan had worked. They knew that the wax had come from a magic candle, so could only be washed away by someone with a pure and good heart—someone like Astrid.

"I will marry you instead!" the Prince said to Astrid and, because his cruel stepmother, the Queen, had agreed to the test, there was nothing she could do about it. The curse of the White Bear was lifted! The troll princess was so angry, she vanished in a puff of green smoke. Astrid and her Prince were married that very day...

... in the castle that lay east of the sun and west of the moon.

The Magic Gifts

There was once a young lad who lived with his mother in a shabby little cottage somewhere not far from where you live.

One night, the lad's mother was feeling poorly, so he offered to make dinner. He popped out to their barn and scooped up a bucket of flour to make some bread with but, when he stepped outside, the North Wind huffed and puffed so hard that the flour blew away. The boy went back into the barn to get more flour, but the same thing happened again and again, until there was no flour left at all.

"Why is the North Wind being so unkind?" groaned the lad. "I'm going to tell him what I think of him!"

So the lad made his mother a broth and set off on the long journey to see the North Wind. He walked and walked until, at last, he came to the house of the North Wind.

When he stepped inside, he found the North Wind reading a book. Plucking up his courage, the lad said, "Good day to you, North Wind."

"What brings you here," asked the North Wind, surprised to have a visitor.

"You came to visit me earlier today," stammered the lad, "and I wondered whether you would be good enough to replace the flour you blew away. You see, we are poor and my mother is ill. If we don't have any flour to bake with, we will starve."

The North Wind thought for a while. "I don't have any flour, but I can give you a special tablecloth. All you need to do is spread it out and say 'Table, be set' and it will serve you a feast of food whenever you need it."

The lad was delighted with his gift, so he thanked the North Wind and set off for home again.

Night soon began to fall, so the lad decided to stay at an inn on his way home. He didn't have any money to pay the landlady for a room, so he laid his magic tablecloth on a table and muttered, "Table, be set."

In the blink of an eye, a magnificent feast appeared before him. There was enough to feed all the guests and the staff. The landlady was so delighted that she gave the lad a free room for the night. However, when he was fast asleep, she tiptoed into his room and swapped the cloth for one that looked just like it.

The next morning, the lad set off for home with the wrong tablecloth.

When he got there, he didn't waste a second in showing his mother the extraordinary gift the North Wind had given him, but when he said, "Table, be set," not even a crumb appeared before them. His poor mother was dismayed and the lad felt cross with the North Wind for tricking him.

Determined not to be beaten, he again set off on the long journey to the North Wind's house and arrived just before sunset.

"Good evening, North Wind," said the lad.

"Good evening, young man," said the North Wind. "What brings you back here so soon?"

"That tablecloth you gave me didn't work," said the lad, "so I come here once again to ask for the flour you blew away, please."

"Didn't work, eh?" said the North Wind, looking puzzled. "Well, I still don't have any flour, but I can give you my goat," he said, pointing to a billy goat in his garden. "All you have to say is 'Goat, make money' and it will spit out gold coins for you."

The lad thanked the North Wind for his kindness and set off for home.

The moon had risen, so he decided to stay over at the same inn again. He asked the landlady for a room and, to pay his bill, he said to his new billy goat, "Goat, make money." Immediately, the goat spat out two shiny gold coins.

The landlady's eyes lit up at the sight of it and, when the young lad turned in for the night, she sneakily swapped his goat for one from her own stable. The two goats looked exactly the same, so when the lad left the next morning, he had no idea of the mischief she had been up to.

He rushed home to show his mother his new gift from the North Wind but, just like the tablecloth, the goat did nothing. It stood there and bleated. By now, the boy's mother was starting to doubt whether her son was telling the truth, and the lad was growing quite angry with the North Wind. He set off once again for his house.

"Look here," he said, when he got there, "I'm tired of you making a fool of me. I don't want your magic gifts that don't work! All I ask is that you return my flour."

"But I don't have any flour!" huffed the North Wind. "Did you show your gifts to anyone on your way home?"

The lad told him that he had stayed over at an inn. The North Wind smiled. "Well, in that case, I have the ideal gift for you. In the corner, you'll see a big stick. To make it work, say 'Beat, stick, beat' and to make it stop say 'Stop, stick, stop'. That will put things right."

The lad sighed and took the stick. It didn't seem as good as the other gifts

but, after three days of trekking to the North Wind, he was too tired to argue.

On his way home, he stayed at the same inn as before. The landlady was most pleased to see him and offered him a free meal and a room. When she spied the stick in his hand, she was sure that it must be special.

The lad went to bed and, in the early hours, he was woken by the creak of a floorboard. He opened one eye and saw the landlady creep across his room and grab the stick.

Quick as a flash, he leapt up and shouted, "Beat, stick, beat!"

At once, the stick swung at the landlady and she dashed about the room trying to dodge it.

"Make it stop!" she cried, as the stick chased her round in circles. "Make it stop, and I will return your tablecloth and your goat to you!"

And so the lad said, "Stop, stick, stop!" and the stick fell to the floor.

Red in the face, the landlady returned his stolen tablecloth and his goat. The lad set off for home overjoyed that, at last, he could share the magic gifts of the North Wind with his mother. And, my, what a splendid feast they both enjoyed that night.

The Fire Fairy

Deep in the countryside, in the far north of England, there lived a young widow with her playful six-year-old son.

All around their house, there was nothing but hills and moors, and not another soul in sight. Though the widow was sometimes lonely, she kept herself busy looking after their sheep and tending their vegetable patch, and she entertained her son with stories about the fairies and will o' the wisps who were said to live in the nearby glen.

Though the widow loved their home during the day, she had always been afraid of the dark, so as soon as the sun started to set, she lit a roaring fire and tucked herself up in bed, where she could hide under the covers if she got scared.

Her son, however, hated going to bed early and was not at all afraid of the dark.

He liked sitting by the window, looking into the black night, watching mysterious lights flicker across the moors. His mother would nag him to go to bed, but he got so fidgety, he couldn't fall asleep.

One night, when the wind was rattling at the door, his mother urged him to get into bed and stay there.

"There's nowt but mischief and magic on nights like this. The fairies will take you away!" she warned him.

But the boy would not listen. He sat on his little stool by the fire, and his mother went to bed in despair.

Not long after she had fallen asleep, the boy heard a sound coming from the chimney, like a bird fluttering its wings. Suddenly, a tiny girl dropped down and landed right beside him.

She had bright pink hair, sparkling green eyes, sweet rosy cheeks, and pearly little wings.

The Fire Fairy

The boy jumped up off his stool in surprise. "And who might you be?" he asked his unexpected visitor.

"My own self," said the little fairy in a jingly voice and she gave a cheeky smile. "And who are you?"

Not knowing what to answer, the boy mumbled, "My own self too."

The fairy laughed and she and the boy started to play together. First, she used her magic to make the flames of the fire change into amazing shapes, then she gathered the ashes into a pile and turned them into a white horse that pranced round the room, then an oak tree swaying in the breeze, and then dolphins diving through the waves! She even turned the ashes into tiny people who could walk and talk.

The boy's eyes were wide with delight at the fairy's wonderful magic!

Then the fairy breathed on the
ashes and they swirled all around
her, like a tornado. The boy leant
forward to stoke the dwindling fire so
that he could see her better but, as he
did so, a hot cinder jumped out of the
fire and landed on the little fairy's foot.

"Yoww!" squealed the fairy in such a
high-pitched screech that the boy
covered his ears in horror. The scream
went on for so long, the boy feared
that it would wake his mother and he
would get into terrible trouble.

Soon he heard another loud flutter
in the chimney and it scared him so
much, he sprinted across the room

and dived under his bed-covers.
Peeping out, he saw an older fairy
with flame-red hair drop onto the
hearth in front of the fire.

"Who is making such a racket, and
what is all the fuss about?"

"It's my own self, Mother!" wept the
fairy girl. "My foot is burnt and it
hurts!"

"Who did this to you?" said the fairy
mother, looking quite angry.

"Why, it was my own self too!"
sobbed the little fairy.

"Your own self, you say? Well, if you did it to yourself, let's hope you've learnt your lesson!" said the fairy mother and, with that, she took her little fairy girl by the hand and whisked her up the chimney.

The boy sighed with relief, but that night he barely slept a wink, worrying that the fairy mother would come back and tell him off. And the following night, when his mother told him to go to bed early, he didn't argue at all—much to his mother's surprise, he was under his blankets in the blink of an eye.

Playing with fairies, he had discovered, was a great deal of fun, but playing with fire causes nothing but trouble.

Snow White
and the Seven Dwarfs

Once upon a time, a beautiful baby girl was born to a king and queen. She had lips as red as blood, hair as black as night, and skin as white as snow, and so they called her Snow White.

Not long after Snow White was born, the queen died and her father took a new wife. Snow White's stepmother was beautiful, but she was also vain, and she owned a magic mirror. Every morning, when she got up, she would stand before her magic mirror and ask:

"Mirror, mirror on the wall,
Who is the fairest of them all?"

Without fail, the mirror would reply, "You, my queen, are the fairest of them all," and the queen's vanity would be satisfied.

For many years, the mirror answered the same way.

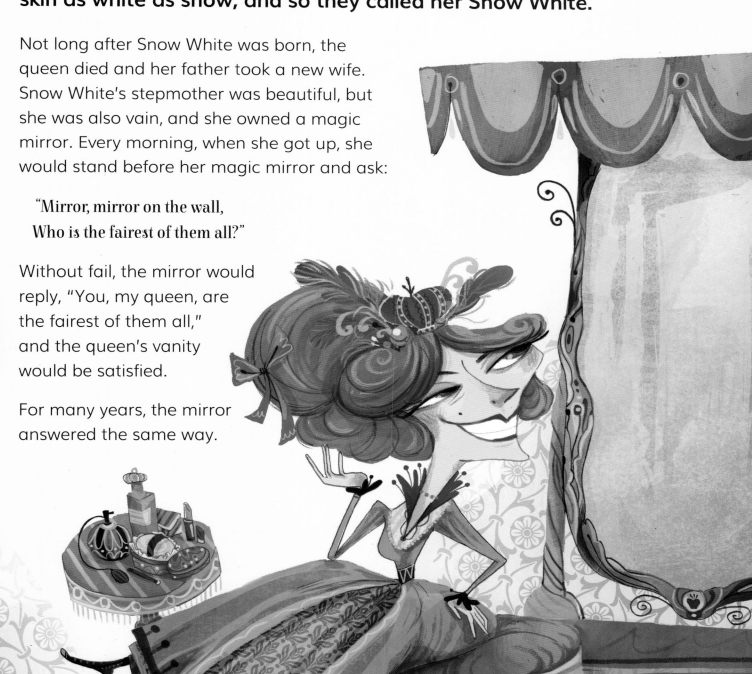

But the day after Snow White's sixteenth birthday, the mirror answered:

> "You, my queen, are fair. It's true,
> But Snow White is even fairer than you!"

The queen was enraged and, from that moment, whenever she looked at Snow White, her heart swelled with envy.

In time, her hatred grew so great, she couldn't even bear to look at Snow White, so she summoned a huntsman.

"Take Snow White into the woods and kill her," demanded the queen. "And bring her heart to me as proof."

The next day, the huntsman took Snow White into the woods to kill her, but, when he saw her frightened face, he hesitated. Snow White began to cry.

"Please let me live," she begged him. "What have I done wrong?"

The huntsman told Snow White about the queen's orders and, taking pity on her, he said, "Run into the woods, and don't let the queen see you ever again."

He watched her run away, then he killed a deer and took its heart to the palace. The wicked queen was so pleased, she asked the cook to roast it for her dinner.

Now Snow White was all alone. She felt so afraid that she ran as fast as she could—over gnarled roots and jagged rocks and past thorny bushes—until she came upon a charming little house.

She looked through the window and saw a little table set with seven candles, seven little plates, seven little knives and forks, and seven little cups. In the middle of the table, there was fresh bread and cheese, and bowls of fruit and vegetables. At the back of the room, there stood seven little beds.

Snow White called out, but there was nobody home. She stepped inside and realized how terribly hungry and thirsty she felt. "I'm sure they won't mind if I have a little bite to eat," she thought, and she helped herself to some food. Then, she felt so tired, she tried the beds. "I'm sure they won't mind if I take a little nap," she yawned, and she quickly fell into a deep sleep.

Soon, the owners of the little house returned—they were seven dwarfs, who had been mining gold in the mountains all day.

When they lit their candles, they saw that someone had been in their house.

The first dwarf said, "Who's been sitting in my chair?"

The second dwarf said, "Who's been sipping my juice?"

The third dwarf said, "Who's been eating our bread?"

The fourth dwarf said, "Who's been nibbling our cheese?"

The fifth dwarf said, "Who's been munching our fruit?"

The sixth dwarf said, "Who's been eating our vegetables?"

Finally, the seventh dwarf said, "Who's this lying here on my bed?"

And they found Snow White

curled up and fast asleep.

Snow White looked so peaceful, the good-hearted dwarfs didn't want to disturb her, so they let her sleep.

When she awoke in the morning and saw the dwarfs, Snow White was startled, but they were so kind and friendly that she soon told them who she was and how the wicked queen had planned to kill her.

The dwarfs were worried for Snow White, so they invited her to stay with them. In return, Snow White took care of their house and cooked for them. For many months, they were very happy like this and, every day, when the dwarfs left for work, they warned her, "Remember: don't open the door to anyone, Snow White!"

⁂

Back at the castle, the wicked queen hadn't used her magic mirror for some time. But, one day, she enquired,

"Mirror, mirror on the wall,
Who is the fairest of them all?"

Imagine her horror when the magic mirror answered:

"You, my queen, are fair. It's true,
But Snow White with the seven dwarfs
is still fairer than you!"

The wicked queen was furious that the huntsman had deceived her! She ordered her guards to track down Snow White and the seven dwarfs, then she disguised herself as a sweet old lady. With a basket of poisoned apples, she knocked at their door, calling, "Apples! Rosy apples for sale!"

Through the window, Snow White spied a smiling old lady with a basket of the rosiest-looking apples she had ever seen. She was tempted to let her in, but remembered the dwarfs' advice.

"I'm sorry, I can't open the door to you," Snow White called out.

"Don't worry, dear," said the old lady, "I'll pass you an apple through the window. You may have it as a gift."

Snow White hesitated, then opened the window. The old lady picked a beautiful apple from the basket that was half red and half green.

"I'll share it with you," said the old lady, slicing the apple down the middle. She took a bite from the green half and handed the red half to Snow White.

Snow White took a bite and no sooner had it touched her lips than she fell to the floor. The queen threw off her disguise and laughed cruelly.

"At last! Now let's see who's the fairest of them all!" she cackled, and she left Snow White lying there—her envious heart at peace at last.

When the seven dwarfs returned that night, they despaired to see Snow White with the poisoned apple at her side. They did all they could to bring the princess back to life, but she was as still and quiet as a statue.

"We shall make a glass coffin for her," wept the dwarfs. So that is what they did and, for a year and a day, Snow White lay in the glass coffin outside the house of the seven dwarfs. In all that time, her blood-red lips and snow-white skin never changed.

Now it just happened one day that a prince came riding through the forest and found the coffin. When he saw Snow White inside it, he fell so madly in love that he couldn't leave. When the dwarfs came home and told him what had happened, the prince was horrified. After that, he visited Snow White every day, and soon asked the dwarfs if he could take her coffin with him to his palace. They agreed.

The next day, the prince brought his servants to help him carry the glass coffin. But, when they lifted it up, the coffin jolted and a piece of poisoned apple, which had been stuck in Snow White's throat, came loose. Much to everyone's surprise, Snow White opened her eyes, yawned and asked, "Where am I?"

The dwarfs jumped up and down with joy, and the happy prince invited Snow White to come and stay with him at his palace for her own safety.

The prince and Snow White soon fell in love and agreed to marry. But, while the wicked queen was still out there, the prince feared for Snow White's life, so he came up with a secret plan. He invited the queen to their wedding.

The queen was delighted to get a wedding invitation and, before she left for the celebration, she stood before her magic mirror and asked,

"Mirror, mirror on the wall,
Who is the fairest of them all?"

And the mirror replied,

"You, my queen, are fair. It's true,
But the princess you'll see is fairer than you!"

Wild with anger, the queen threw the mirror to the floor, smashing it into a thousand pieces. "What princess is this?" she raged. And her heart was, once more, flooded with envy.

When the wicked queen arrived at the wedding and saw Snow White sitting on the throne, she screamed, "YOU!"

At this, the prince's guards dashed around her and clamped her in irons. As her punishment, the vain queen was thrown into a dungeon, which was covered from floor to ceiling in mirrors.

With the queen locked away at last, Snow White and the prince were able to live happily ever after.

Fate Finds a Fish

There was once a rich Baron in the north of England who could see into the future. When his only son was a toddler, the Baron decided to see what the boy's future held in store for him. To his horror, he saw that his son would grow up to marry a poor and lowly maid, who had just been born within the walls of the city.

The Baron wanted better for his son, so he called for his horse and he set out to search the city until he could track down the home of the newborn girl.

He eventually found a tired-looking man sitting on a doorstep with his head in his hands. The Baron asked him what was wrong and the man replied, "My lord, our sixth daughter has just been born. I am so poor, I can't afford to feed her!"

"Don't despair!" said the Baron. "I will take away your sixth child and raise it as my own child, so you don't have to worry."

The man was grateful for the Baron's kindness. He carried out a basket with a sweet baby girl inside and handed it to the Baron, who rode away at great speed. But the Baron had no intention of caring for the baby. Instead, he rode to the river and tossed the basket into it, with the baby inside—then he galloped home again.

However, the basket didn't sink. It bobbed along the river and washed up outside the cottage of a humble fisherman. He found it and took pity on the baby girl. The fisherman named her Alice and, over the next sixteen years, she blossomed into a hard-working and lovely young woman.

One day, it so happened that the Baron and his friends were hunting along the river and they stopped at the fisherman's cottage for a drink. Alice served the men and they all noticed her great beauty. "Who do you think she'll marry?" one of the men asked the Baron.

"I'll look into her future," boasted the Baron. "Come here, girl! Tell me, when were you born?"

"I don't know, sir," said Alice. "My father found me washed up in a basket sixteen years ago."

The Baron's face turned pale with shock— he knew straight away who she was. He made an excuse and left in a hurry, but he rode back to the cottage later that day and handed Alice a sealed letter.

"I have come to make your fortune," said the Baron. "Take this letter to my brother in Scarborough and he will ensure you have a happy life."

Alice thought that fate must be on her side. She said farewell to her father, and set out with the letter in her hand. What she didn't know was what the Baron had written. The letter said:

"Dear brother, Please take the young bearer of this letter and put her to her death today."

On her way to Scarborough, Alice stopped over at an inn. On that very night, a band of robbers broke in. When they crept into her room, they found no money, but they did open

and read her letter from the Baron. Now, the chief of the robbers knew the Baron and didn't like him at all. Feeling sorry for the girl, he took a fresh sheet of paper and wrote:

"Dear brother, Please take the young bearer of this letter and marry her to my son today."

The next morning, Alice walked on to Scarborough with the letter in her hand and no idea what it said. When she found the castle of the Baron's brother, she presented the letter to him and was surprised when he gave orders for a wedding to be prepared at once—she was to marry William, the Baron's son! Alice and William were married that very day and were given a special gift of golden rings.

A month went by and it became clear that the young couple were a match made in heaven. But soon, the Baron arrived and, when he discovered what had happened, he was enraged. His plan had somehow been foiled!

He invited Alice for a walk along the cliffs, but when they got there, he tried to push her over the cliff. Alice fought him and begged for her life.

"Why are you doing this?" she cried. "I have done you no harm! Please spare me and I will do whatever you wish."

"Very well," said the Baron, and he grabbed her golden wedding ring and threw it into the sea. "I don't wish to see you ever again unless you can show me that ring!" With that, he let her go.

Poor Alice couldn't return to William, so she walked until she came to the house of a great nobleman, where she found work as a scullery maid. Alice worked there for many months with a deep sadness in her heart.

Then, one fateful day, she spied the Baron and William arriving for a great banquet. She longed to run to her husband, but she feared what the Baron would do, so she went back to her work, feeling downhearted.

The cook was so busy, she asked Alice to prepare the fish. As Alice cleaned it, she saw something shiny glinting in its mouth. Alice saw that it was her wedding ring—the very one the Baron had cast into the sea!

With her heart pounding with excitement, Alice cooked up the fish as best as she could—just how her father had taught her—and she slipped the golden wedding ring on to her finger.

When the fish came to the dining table, the guests thought it was the best dish of the banquet and they wanted to thank the person who had cooked it.

The nobleman sent word down to the kitchen and the cook told Alice to wash and tidy herself before she went up into the banqueting hall. Alice took a deep breath and nervously walked into the room.

The guests were surprised to see such a young cook, but when the Baron

saw that it was Alice, he was fit to burst with rage! Alice quickly showed him the gold wedding ring on her finger and told him about the fish.

The Baron knew then that he could fight fate no longer—no matter how hard he tried, he could not change the future he had seen all those years ago. He called for an extra seat and introduced everyone to his son's wife, Alice. The Baron vowed never to tamper with fate again, and from that day on...

Alice and William were very happy together.

The Changelings

There was once a husband and his wife who were lucky enough to have adorable baby twins. They loved their babies with all their hearts and doted on the sweet duo.

One day, the woman was called upon by a friend. "Please can you help me?" wailed the friend. "I've locked myself out and I need a leg-up to get through my window."

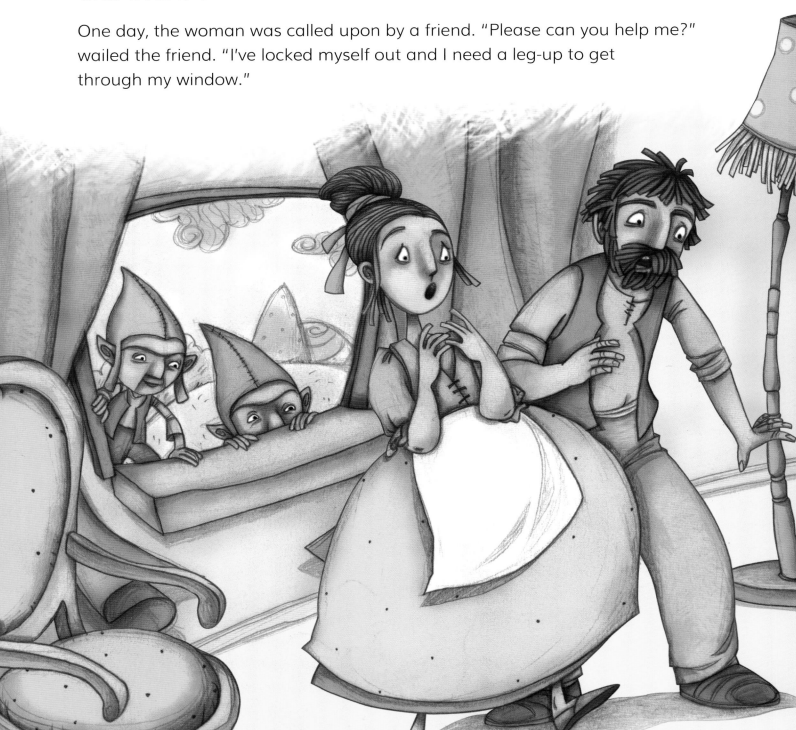

The woman didn't like to leave her little ones alone, but they were both sound asleep in their cots, so she rushed to help her friend.

However, on her way back, she saw two strange little men walking away from her house. They had elfin ears and green shoes with pointed toes. They both sported mischievous smiles.

Alarmed, the woman rushed back to check on her babies, but they were both still lying there, tucked up in bed, deep in their baby dreams.

A few months went by, though, and the husband and wife began to think that something was wrong with their babies. They hadn't grown an inch, but their faces looked old and wrinkly, and they cried all day and night. No matter how hard the couple tried, they couldn't comfort them.

"There's mischief going on here, I'm sure of it," said the husband in despair. "I don't think these babies are ours. I think the fairies swapped them for their own. I think they're changelings!"

The wife wept to think of her babies as changelings, but she suspected that what her husband had said was true.

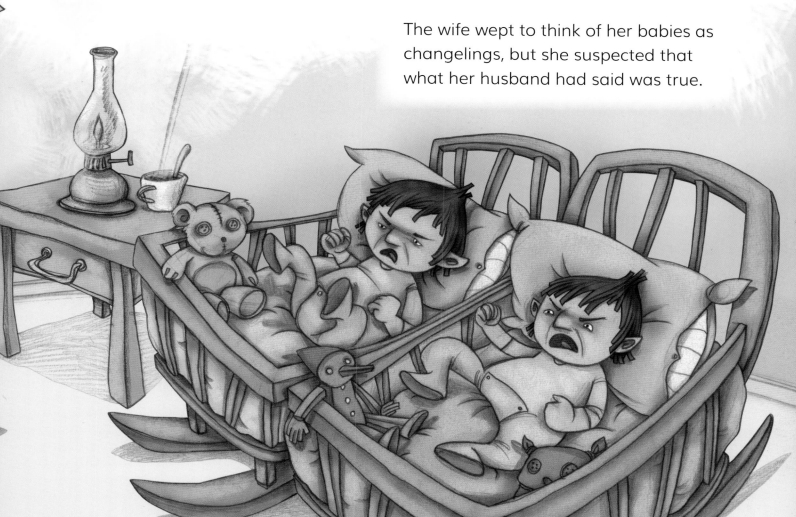

The next day, she set out to see the wise woman who lived in the next village and told her all her fears.

"There's only one way to know," said the wise woman. "Fetch two dozen hen's eggs, crack them and keep only the shells. Boil a pot of water on the fire and, when it's bubbling away, throw in the eggshells and stir. You'll soon find out whether your babies are changelings or not."

As odd as the instructions sounded, the woman did exactly as she was told. All the time, the twins lay crying in their cots, their wrinkled little faces watching her every move. Just as she threw the eggshells into the bubbling water, they both sat bolt upright and, in old men's voices, cried out:

"What are you doing? We've seen potatoes boil and carrots simmer, but never a dinner of eggshells!"

The woman jumped in surprise to hear the two babies talk like that and, quick as she could, she scooped a changeling under each arm, then ran down the lane to where a little wooden bridge ran over a river. She dangled the wrinkled elfins over the water and cried out, "Give me back my own fair babies, or I'll drop these changelings in the river!"

At that, the two elves she had seen many months before suddenly appeared on the bridge and snatched the changelings away from her. Just as quickly as they had appeared, they vanished again.

The woman ran all the way home again and, as she burst through the front door, she was overjoyed to hear the cute chuckles of her own babies. There they were, tucked up in their cots, as chubby-cheeked and beautiful as the day they had been taken away from her. As she leant down to cuddle them, the twins looked up and, together, they gurgled their very first word: "Mama!"

Atlanta and the Golden Apples

Long ago in Ancient Greece, a king called Iasus longed for a son to inherit his throne, so when the queen had a baby girl, the disappointed king took the poor baby away and left it in the wilderness.

The baby, whose name was Atlanta, was found by a mother bear, who took pity on her and raised her with her own cubs until, one day, a kind hunter came by. Thinking Atlanta was all alone, the hunter took her to his home. He taught Atlanta the skills she needed to survive in the wild and, with his help, she grew up to be a great hunter—she was fearless, strong, fast, and highly skilled with a bow.

Atlanta's skills were soon noticed by Artemis, the goddess of the wild. Artemis and Atlanta became good friends, and Artemis warned Atlanta that she should never marry, or she would lose her incredible powers.

Artemis wasn't the only one who had heard of Atlanta—when stories spread of the young woman's courage and strength, she was challenged to fights, invited on perilous voyages, and asked to hunt a giant boar that terrorized the land. She succeeded in everything she tried her hand at and, when King Iasus learned of her story, he soon realized that this incredible woman must be the daughter he had left in the wild.

Accepting that Atlanta was as brave as any son and feeling great regret, he invited her to return home and begged for her forgiveness. Atlanta agreed, but she hadn't been reunited with her family for very long, when her father began to nag her to get married.

Atlanta was happy as she was and, remembering Artemis's warning, she made a deal with him.

"Father, I will only marry the man who can beat me in a race, and anyone who fails must be thrown into prison."

Atlanta was certain that no man would be foolish enough to risk jail for her, but she hadn't realized how widely she was admired. As soon as people heard of Atlanta's challenge, men were lining up to race against her. Of course, Atlanta won every race with ease, because she was one of the fastest humans on the planet.

Just as Atlanta was reaching the point when she could bear to race no more, a young man called Melanion came forward and requested a race. He was handsome and witty, and he had fallen in love with Atlanta.

When Atlanta met him, she liked him so much that she didn't want to race him, but she had no choice but to accept his challenge. A date was set for their contest.

Desperate to marry Atlanta, Melanion prayed at the temple of Aphrodite—the goddess of love—and begged for her help winning the race. The goddess Aphrodite had long wished

that headstrong Atlanta would find love, so she took pity on Melanion. She appeared before him and offered him a gift of three golden apples—each one was enchanted.

"Throw these down as you race with Atlanta and she will run after them. If you are quick, you will be able to get ahead of her. If you succeed, you must bring me a gift to thank me."

Melanion thanked Aphrodite and vowed he would return to her temple.

On the day of the race, he concealed the apples inside his tunic.

When the contest began, Atlanta gracefully powered ahead, but they hadn't gone far when Melanion threw a golden apple ahead of her. Atlanta saw a glint of gold from the corner of her eye and, wondering what it could be, she ran over to it. It was a thing of great beauty but, as she grabbed the golden apple, Melanion caught up with her and flashed a smile at her.

Alarmed at his speed, Atlanta raced alongside him and soon overtook him again. Just as she did so, Melanion threw down a second apple. Atlanta saw the flash of gold whoosh by and, though she knew it must be another golden apple, she found herself unable to resist it. She ran over to it, and Melanion bolted into the lead.

Atlanta dashed back onto the track and gave chase again, but just as she drew level with Melanion and as the finish line came into sight, Melanion hurled down the third and final golden apple.

Atlanta roared with frustration, as she couldn't control her desire to pick it up. She sprinted over to the magic apple and grabbed it, but as she stood up to race again, Melanion crossed the finish line. Proud Atlanta had lost the race.

Atlanta and Melanion were married a week later. Despite the fact that Atlanta had never wanted to marry,

they made a fine couple and were happy together—so happy, in fact, that Melanion completely forgot to bring the gift of thanks he had promised to the goddess Aphrodite.

He soon discovered that it isn't wise to offend the gods. One day, when he and Atlanta were out walking, an angry Aphrodite appeared before the happy couple and turned them both into lions. Atlanta and Melanion were forced to flee into the wild, where they hunted together for the rest of their lives.

The Fairy Bride

It is true that fairies love beautiful things—beautiful flowers, beautiful trees, and, most of all, beautiful people. None more so than Finvara, the fairy king, who was famed for whisking away pretty girls to live in his fairy palace, hidden among the green hills of Ireland.

Once there, he enchanted them with sweet fairy music so that they completely forgot their homes and their loved ones.

Now, a young lord named Rory O'Connor lived near Finvara, and the two were old friends. Lord O'Connor had recently married a beautiful girl called Ethna, who was as bright and kind as she was pretty. With long auburn locks, sparkling green eyes, and fair skin, she was the loveliest bride in the land.

O'Connor was besotted with his bride and, every day, he held celebrations to show his love for her. From morning till night, there was music and dancing and feasting. The court had never seen such grand and happy times.

One evening, following a merry feast, Ethna was twirling gracefully across the ballroom in a gown of golden gossamer, when she collapsed on the floor in a dead faint.

O'Connor tried all he could to wake her, but Ethna lay perfectly still— nothing could stir her. He carried her to bed and asked an old maid to keep a watchful eye over his bride. But tiredness soon got the better of the old maid and she too fell asleep.

When the maid awoke in the morning, she was horrified to see that Ethna had disappeared. She quickly roused the lord, who frantically searched the castle and its grounds, but his bride was nowhere to be seen. Desperate for help, O'Connor rode his fastest horse to the home of Finvara, the fairy king. Perhaps his old friend's magic could help him?

Halfway there, he stopped to rest his horse when he heard wispy voices on the breeze. O'Connor was standing beneath the path of some fairies on their way to see Finvara.

"Finvara will be happy now," he heard one of them say. "He has the beautiful Ethna in his palace at last. She'll soon have forgotten all about her husband."

"Poor O'Connor," said another small voice. "He was Finvara's friend. If only he knew that he could dig into the hill to save his bride. But, it is hard work and Finvara's magic is so strong!"

O'Connor was standing beneath the path of some fairies...

"We'll see about that!" exclaimed O'Connor. "Not even the fairy king can stand between me and my wife!"

As quickly as he could, O'Connor rode back to his castle and gathered a gang of men, armed with spades. Together, they set out for Finvara's fairy hill and began to dig through it. The men dug the hard earth all day, making a huge trench in the middle of the hill. When the sun finally set, they left, feeling tired to the bone.

However, when they returned the next day, the hill looked like it had never been touched—the soil and the lush green grass were back in place. Fairy magic was at work!

Lord O'Connor was determined not to be beaten so, again, he and his men set to work and dug a new trench —this time, even deeper and wider. But when they returned the next day, the hill had been restored to normal.

This went on for three more days and, each day, O'Connor grew more weary and despairing—he was no nearer to saving his beloved Ethna.

Just as the young lord had lost all hope, he heard a small, familiar fairy voice whisper in his ear:

"Sprinkle the trench you have dug with salt, and your hard work will be safe from Finvara's magic."

That night, O'Connor and his men sprinkled salt all over their freshly dug trench. The next morning, they were amazed to see that the trick had worked—the trench was still there. Now they worked even harder than before—at last, Finvara's hidden fairy palace felt within their reach. Indeed, when they put their ears close to the ground, they could just make out the sound of sweet fairy music.

"We are close now, Finvara!" shouted O'Connor. "Give up my bride if you wish your palace to be safe!"

All was silent until, suddenly, a clear voice rang out from the hill.

"Lay down your spades and I will return Ethna. I, Finvara the fairy king, have spoken!"

O'Connor put down his spade and waited nervously. At last, a door appeared in the side of the hill and out stepped Ethna, looking more beautiful than ever. O'Connor gently carried her to his horse and rode like the wind back to his castle.

However, the young lord soon found that, when he spoke to Ethna, she couldn't answer him or even smile at him—she was still under Finvara's enchantment! O'Connor was enraged. If only he could break the spell!

Once again, in his moment of need, a little fairy whisper came to his aid:
"To break the spell, find the enchanted pin in your bride's dress. Pull it out,
bury it deep where nobody will ever find it and your Ethna will return to you."

O'Connor rushed back to his bride and hastily searched for the pin. He finally
found a tiny silver pin buried in the folds of Ethna's dress. He hid it beneath a
thorn tree in the castle grounds, where it could never be discovered.

He rushed back to his wife just in time to hear her call his name, and he was
so happy that he kissed her. In that moment, all the memories of Ethna's life
came rushing back to her, and her fairyland adventure faded to a dream.

Mischievous Finvara never bothered the newlyweds again but, to this day,
there is a hill in Knockma in Ireland with a great trench cut out of the middle.

They call it Fairy's Glen

Jack and the Beanstalk

Once upon a time, there was a poor widow who had an only son called Jack. They lived in a tiny cottage and all they owned in the world was a cow called Milky-White.

Every morning, Jack took a pail of milk from Milky-White to sell at the market. But Milky-White was getting old and, one morning, she stopped giving milk.

Jack's mother despaired, for without the milk to sell, they had no money for food.

"You'll have to take Milky-White to the market and sell her," she told Jack. "And be sure to get a good price!"

So off Jack went, leading the cow behind him. He hadn't gone too far, when he met an old man.

"Good morning, Jack!" said the old man.

Jack wondered how the old man knew his name.

"Where are you off to with this fine cow?" the old man enquired.

Jack explained about Milky-White.

The old man looked thoughtful. "What do you say to a trade? If you can tell me how many beans make five, I'll do a fair swap with you."

Jack answered quickly. "Two in each hand and one in the mouth—that's how many beans make five!"

"Well done, Jack!" said the old man. "You're a smart boy, indeed. Here are the beans themselves." And the old man pulled some strange-looking beans from his pocket. "I'll trade these for your cow."

"Ha! No, thank you," said Jack. "That's not a fair swap!"

"Ah, but you see," said the old man, "these beans are magic beans. If you plant them today, you'll have the best beanstalks in the world tomorrow!"

Jack thought that sounded good, so he decided to take the magic beans. He handed over Milky-White and set off for home again.

His mother was surprised to see him back so soon. "Did you get a good price for the cow?" she asked.

Jack told his mother about the swap he had made for the magic beans and she flew into a rage. "You gave away our cow for these beans?" she cried. "What were you thinking?"

And, with that, she threw the beans out of the window and sent Jack to bed without any supper.

The next morning, when Jack woke up, his room looked darker than usual. He opened his curtains to find a giant beanstalk outside. The beans were magic, after all!

Jack quickly got dressed and began to climb the beanstalk. He climbed and climbed until at last he reached the top, which was just above the clouds. He stepped onto a road and followed it all the way to an enormous castle.

As he approached the castle, he could smell food. Jack's tummy rumbled with hunger—he hadn't eaten any breakfast before he had left.

He banged on the castle door and it was answered by a giantess, who didn't see Jack, as he was so small.

"Down here!" he cried to get her attention.

The giantess jumped when she saw him. "What are you doing here? Don't you know my husband is a giant who eats little boys?"

"Oh, please don't let him eat me!" said Jack. "I've come so far and I'm so hungry. Please could you spare me some food?"

The giantess took pity on Jack and carried him to the kitchen, where she gave him a hunk of bread and some cheese. Jack was eating when suddenly the castle shook with the thud of giant footsteps.

"Oh my!" said the giantess. "I can't let my husband find you here! Quick—jump into my apron pocket!" And she hid Jack away.

Jack peeped out of her pocket to see a huge, grumpy-looking giant walk into the kitchen, holding three cows by the ankles.

"Wife, I am hungry," he said, "Cook these for lunch." Then he stopped and sniffed the air, and growled...

"Fee Fi Fo Fum!
I smell the **blood** of an Englishman.
Be he **alive** or be he **dead**,

Scared, Jack ducked his head inside the pocket and the giantess said, "You must be mistaken, dear. Perhaps you can smell the clothes of the boy you ate yesterday? Now go and rest and I'll bring you lunch."

The giant thudded out of the kitchen and Jack leapt out of the apron pocket. He was about to run away, but the giant's wife stopped him.

"He'll smell you," she said. "Wait until he has his nap after lunch."

So the giantess served her hungry husband a huge lunch, and Jack waited anxiously for him to finish.

However, when the giant's plate was empty, instead of napping, he took out some bags of gold and began to count his coins. Eventually, his eyes grew heavy and he fell asleep. The giant began to snore.

Jack couldn't believe how much gold the giant had and, unable to resist, he quickly heaved a moneybag over his shoulder and dragged it out of the castle to the top of the beanstalk, and all the way back home again.

His mother had been out of her mind with worry about him and she was waiting for him at the bottom.

Jack dropped the bag of gold coins before her and said, "See, mother. Wasn't I right about the beans?" At that, his mother danced a happy jig!

Though they had enough gold to last them a long time, Jack was an adventurous lad and he couldn't wait to climb the beanstalk again.

A few days later, up he went and, this time, when he reached the giant's castle, the giantess was busy sweeping the doorstep.

"Good morning!" said Jack politely. "The food you gave me the other day was so delicious, could you spare me some more, please?"

"You silly boy for coming back!" she said. "Go away now, or the giant will eat you up! He's very grumpy because he's lost one of his moneybags."

But she took pity on Jack, as he was so small and thin, and she carried him to the kitchen. Jack was about to start eating when the thud of giant footsteps came stomping along the hallway. Quick as a flash, Jack hid in a cupboard.

The giant entered the room, sniffed the air and boomed:

"Fee Fi Fo Fum!
I smell the blood of an Englishman.
Be he alive or be he dead,
I'll grind his bones to make my bread!"

"Nonsense!" said his wife. "You must be imagining things!" And she told him to go and wait for his lunch.

This time, when the giant finished eating, he asked his wife to bring him his golden hen. She put it on the dining table before him and the giant said "Lay!" The hen clucked and laid an egg of solid gold! Jack couldn't believe his eyes.

The giant held the egg tightly in his hands, closed his eyes and soon fell fast asleep.

Jack tiptoed up to the dining table, grabbed the hen and sprinted out of the room. But as he reached the castle door, the hen began to squawk.

As Jack ran to the beanstalk, he heard the giant shouting, "Wife! Wife! Where is my golden hen?"

Jack dashed down the beanstalk as swiftly as he could. When he reached the bottom, he called his mother to show her the golden hen.

Jack said "Lay!" and, just as it had for the giant, the hen laid a golden egg! Jack's mother was delighted—now they would always have money whenever they needed it!

But Jack's adventures weren't over yet! He wanted to climb the beanstalk again. A few days later, up he went.

This time, Jack crept into the castle's kitchen through an open window. The giantess was preparing lunch and didn't see him. Soon he heard the thud of the giant's footsteps, so he quickly ducked behind a bucket.

The giant entered the room, sniffed the air and roared:

"Fee Fi Fo Fum!
I smell the blood of an Englishman.
Be he alive or be he dead,
I'll grind his bones to make my bread!"

"Well, of course you can!" laughed the giantess. "You can smell the clothes of the lad you ate for dinner last night!"

But the giant felt sure he could smell a fresh boy, so he searched the cupboards and even looked inside the oven, but he didn't find Jack.

The giant gave up and, as he had the other days, he went off to eat his giant lunch. Afterwards, he asked his wife to bring him his magic harp.

She set it on the dining table and the giant said, "Sing!" Straight away, the magic harp started to sing a beautiful melody. Soon, the giant drifted into a deep and peaceful sleep.

Jack thought the harp was amazing, so he tiptoed across the dining table, grabbed it and ran for the door. But the harp cried out, "Master! Master!"

The giant woke up just in time to see Jack running out of the door. Jack ran as fast as his legs could carry him, but, thanks to his huge strides, the giant soon started to catch up.

With his heart pounding and the giant close behind, Jack leapt onto the beanstalk and nimbly slid all the way down.

The giant climbed onto the beanstalk too, but it shook and shuddered under his great weight. He was so big and clumsy, he just couldn't keep up.

When Jack reached the bottom, he grabbed an axe and he chopped and chopped at the beanstalk with all his strength. Soon, the stalk wobbled, swayed and snapped in two, bringing the boy-eating giant crashing to the ground. The giant was killed in an instant!

From that day on, all the boys in the kingdom were safe, and Jack and his mother were never poor again, thanks to the hen that laid golden eggs and the magical singing harp, which people came from far and wide to see.

The Farmer and the Boggart

In the village of Mumby in England, there lived a farmer who had just bought a field. The farmer was excited about his new purchase and had lots of grand plans for what he'd grow there.

As soon as he could, he set off to work his field and prepare it for planting. But when he was halfway through the job, a hairy little fellow leapt out from the hedgerow, shaking his fist angrily. He had a shaggy beard, eyes as big as saucers, and he smelt like rotten eggs! He was a boggart.

"What do you think
you're doing on my land?"
the boggart yelled at the farmer.

Now the boggart didn't really own the field, he lived in the marshes nearby, but boggarts are cantankerous types, and this boggart was in the mood for getting up to no good.

"What do you mean?" cried the farmer, surprised to find a stinky boggart standing before him. "This is my field—I bought it fair and square!"

"Well, I've lived here all my life," lied the boggart. "I own this field and I'll ruin whatever you plant here." And he stamped his feet and scowled.

However, the farmer wasn't easily fooled. He knew that boggarts were terrible mischief-makers. He thought for a second.

"I tell you what," said the farmer. "Let's make a deal. I'll plant the field and share the crop with you—half for you, half for me. How does that sound?"

The boggart grumpily agreed to the deal but, deep down, he was amazed at his good luck—nobody had ever given in this easily before!

"Right," said the farmer. "Which half of the crop would you like to have? The half below ground or the half above ground?"

"Why, the half above ground, of course!" said the boggart, thinking the farmer a complete fool for asking.

And so the boggart went on his way, and the farmer dug rows in his field and planted it with potatoes.

When the potatoes were ready to be harvested, the boggart came to collect his half of the crop.

"Here you go!" smiled the farmer. "The half above ground, as you asked." And he gave the boggart a wheelbarrow of leafy tops.

The boggart saw the farmer's big, heavy sacks of potatoes and he stamped his feet with frustration.

"What would you like next time?" asked the farmer. "Above or below?"

"Below!" demanded the boggart—he wasn't going to get caught out again! Once he'd marched away, the clever farmer started to plant some wheat.

When the wheat was ready to be harvested, the farmer took the golden grains, and he left the roots—which were below ground—for the boggart.

The boggart shook his fists with rage at being tricked again.

"Right!" he cried. "Plant wheat again, but this time, no above or below ground! We get half a field each!"

The farmer did exactly as the boggart said but, the night before the harvest, he sneaked into the boggart's half of the field and hid lots of iron bars in the ground around the wheat stalks.

The next day, the boggart turned up with his scythe and started to cut the wheat but, within minutes, his scythe hit an iron bar and snapped in two. The boggart was absolutely furious!

He jumped up and down until he was quite red in the face.

"You can keep your stupid field!" he shouted—and the boggart stormed off, shaking his fists as he went.

Much to the farmer's relief, he never saw that troublesome boggart ever again—and his field grew brilliant and bountiful harvests every year!

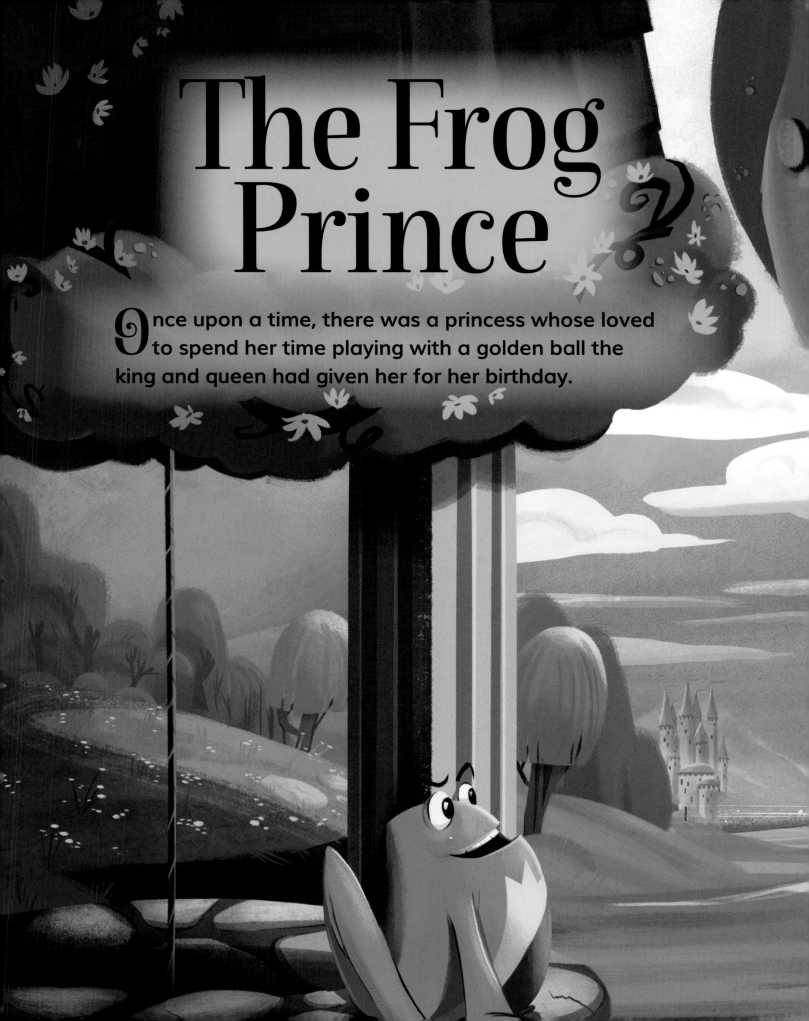

The Frog Prince

Once upon a time, there was a princess whose loved to spend her time playing with a golden ball the king and queen had given her for her birthday.

One day, the princess was playing in the palace gardens, when she threw the ball up high, and it landed—splash!—in an old well. The princess ran to fetch her ball, but the well was so dark and deep, she couldn't see a thing down there.

"Oh, what a fool I am!" she cried. "I'd give anything to get my golden ball back! My jewels, my clothes, my crown... anything!"

Just then, a frog stuck its head out of the murky water and croaked, "You say 'anything', princess?"

The princess leapt back, startled. "Yes, anything! But I can't see how a frog like you can help me."

"I don't want your jewels or clothes, but if I fetch your golden ball, will you take me home with you and let me dine with you and eat from your plate? Will you let me sleep in your bed?"

The princess was revolted by the idea of dining and sleeping with a frog, but she desperately wanted her ball.

"I'm sure he's just joking," she thought. "Yes, whatever, just please get my golden ball for me!" she said.

So the frog dived into the dark depths of the well and fetched her toy. When he reappeared a few minutes later, he dropped the ball near the princess.

She grabbed it and, without even thanking the frog for his kindness, dashed back to the palace.

"Hey!" cried the frog. "Come back! You were supposed to take me with you!"

But the princess didn't hear his croaks—she was already too far away.

That evening, the princess had just sat down for dinner with her parents when she heard a squelchy noise outside the door, followed by a croaky call: "Princess, you broke your promise. Please let me in!"

The princess opened the door and there was the frog that had saved her ball. Repulsed by the sight of him, she slammed the door and returned to her seat.

"Who was that?" asked the king.

"A revolting talking frog!" said the

176

princess. "It fetched my ball when I lost it in the well earlier and I said it could stay here with me in return."

"Did you make a promise to the frog?" asked the king.

"Yes," said the princess, her cheeks starting to flush red.

"Then you must keep it," said the king. "Open the door right now, young lady."

Feeling a little ashamed of herself, the princess opened the door to the frog and he hopped across the room. When she sat down, he said, "Princess, please let me sit next to you."

The princess squirmed as she picked up the slimy frog and set him down next to her, then she tried to ignore him and began eating her meal.

"Princess, please put me by your plate so that I can eat too," said the frog.

The princess put the frog next to her plate, and looked away in disgust as he flicked out his tongue to eat the rest of her food.

Finally, when everyone had finished eating and chatting, the frog said,

"Princess, please take me up to your

bed and let me sleep there."

The princess jumped out of bed in surprise

The princess knew she had no choice so, feeling quite sick, she carried the frog upstairs and placed him on her satin pillow.

That night, she barely slept a wink, but the frog slept soundly. By morning, the princess was tearful with tiredness. However, when dawn broke, the frog hopped out of bed, down the marble staircase and out through the door.

The princess sighed with relief. "Thank goodness I am rid of that horrible frog!" But that night, just as he had before, he appeared at the palace door again.

Once again, the princess allowed him to sit next to her, eat from her plate, and sleep on her pillow and, once again, the following morning, the frog hopped back to the well.

On the third night, the same happened again—and, by now, the princess was exhausted and angry.

"How I wish I had never spoken to you, you ugly, slimy frog!" she snapped—and she was sure she saw a small tear fall from the frog's eye.

That night, overwhelmed by tiredness, the princess finally gave in and fell asleep next to the frog. When she woke the next morning, she was quite astonished to find a handsome young man lying next to her.

The princess jumped out of bed in surprise, which made the prince laugh. It was such joyful laughter, the princess couldn't help joining in.

"I didn't mean to startle you, princess. I am a prince and I was put under an enchantment by a wicked old fairy. The only way to break her spell was to spend three nights in the company of a princess. I know it must have truly been awful—but thank you so much for saving me."

The princess felt so sorry for being mean to the frog prince, she was extra-nice to him. They chatted for the rest of the day, and the king sent a messenger to the prince's kingdom to tell them the good news.

A few days later, a splendid carriage arrived outside the palace, pulled by eight white horses with fancy plumes.

"I have one last request before I leave," smiled the handsome prince. "Please will you be my wife?"

The princess was delighted and agreed. "But on one condition," she said. "I never have to see a frog again!" And that was the beginning of their long and happy life together.

The Clever Queen

Not so long ago in Greece, there were two brothers—one was very clever and the other was quite foolish—and they inherited a large plot of land.

Half of the land was rich and green and the other half was stony and impossible to farm. Because of this, the two brothers couldn't agree how to divide the land. Tired of arguing with each other, they went to King Demetrius to ask for his advice.

The king decided to test the brothers with some riddles, and he decreed that the brother who gave the best answers would win the good half of the land.

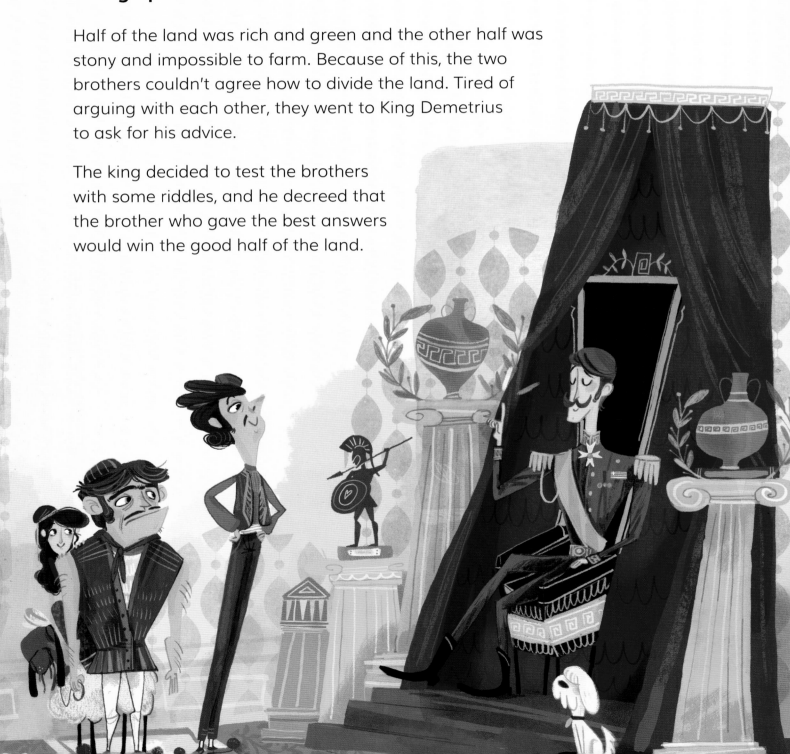

The clever brother smiled smugly, as he loved solving riddles, but the not-so-bright brother despaired.

"Don't worry, Father," said his daughter, Anastasia. "I'll help you." And so she whispered the answers in his ear.

For the king's first riddle, he asked the brothers to name the fastest thing in the world. The clever brother smiled and said, "A peregrine falcon!" But the stupid brother, taking his daughter's advice, answered, "The mind."

For the king's second riddle, he asked them to name the heaviest thing in the world. The clever brother laughed and said, "Iron!" But the stupid brother said, "Fire, because nobody can lift it."

For the king's final riddle, he asked the two to name the most important thing in the world. The clever brother answered, "Money, of course!" But the stupid brother answered, "The ground for, without it, we'd have nothing to stand on."

Impressed by the wisdom of the stupid brother, King Demetrius awarded him the good land and asked him how he got his answers.

As the brother was too honest to lie, he confessed that his daughter, Anastasia, had helped him.

Anastasia, who was hiding behind her father, introduced herself to the king, who was so impressed by her wisdom that he asked her to marry him—and she happily agreed.

On the day of their wedding, King Demetrius issued a strange warning to his new bride.

"I do admire your clever mind, but I must ask you not to meddle in affairs of the crown. If you interfere, I will have to send you home. I hope this never happens, but if it does, you may take one thing from the palace with you—the thing you value most."

A few weeks later, the new queen was walking by the stables when she saw a thief steal a saddle from his friend's horse. The owner spotted him and a loud argument broke out.

"This is a matter for the king!" they cried, but Queen Anastasia stepped forward and named the rightful owner, ending the dispute there and then.

When King Demetrius discovered what had happened, he was upset that his new wife had meddled in his affairs. With a heavy heart, he said she could no longer be his queen.

For Anastasia's last meal with the king, she organised a tremendous feast, and poured enough wine to make him feel quite drowsy. Before long, he fell into a deep sleep at the table.

Queen Anastasia then instructed the palace guards to carry the snoozing king out to the royal carriage and take him with her to her father's farm.

When King Demetrius woke up the next morning to the sound of a cockerel crowing, he was confused.

His new wife just looked at him and smiled. "You said I could take the one thing from the palace that I valued most. I have taken you, my husband. Now, I get to keep you forever."

The king laughed out loud and thanked the heavens for bringing him such a clever queen.

They returned to the palace and, from that day on, King Demetrius and Queen Anastasia looked after their kingdom together.

The Three Wishes

A long time ago, in the middle of a great forest, in a small cabin, there lived a poor woodcutter and his wife. The woodcutter worked long hours felling timber and, though his life was hard, he knew the forest well and he loved it.

Early one morning, he packed his satchel and, axe in hand, he set out into the trees to cut down a mighty oak he had found the day before. He had marked out the tree already and was sure he could get many planks from it to sell to furniture-makers. It would bring the woodcutter and his wife good money.

When he reached the oak tree, he got his axe ready and he swung it back as far as he could. He was about to strike the tree trunk with a powerful blow when he heard a small voice wailing. A little fairy appeared before the oak. She had curly green hair like vines and was wearing a dress made from leaves. In a tiny high voice, she begged the woodcutter to spare the tree.

"This tree is the oldest in the forest," said the fairy. "It is home to many animals and the entrance to our fairyland. I beg you not to harm it."

The woodcutter was greatly surprised to see a fairy before him. Though he had walked a long way for the oak, he was a kind man and took pity on her.

"I will do as you wish," he told the fairy.

"Then I will reward you for your kindness," said the fairy. "I will grant your next three wishes, whatever they may be!" Then the fairy vanished from sight as quickly as she had appeared, leaving the woodcutter wondering whether he might have dreamt it all.

Feeling quite dazed, he slung his axe over his shoulder and went searching for some new trees to cut down, so that his day wasn't wasted.

He chopped and chopped until the daylight started to fade, then he began the long trek home through the forest. All the way back, he puzzled over the fairy and convinced himself that he must have imagined the whole thing.

As darkness fell, the air became so icy that the woodcutter was quite glad to get back to his cabin. His wife had set a roaring fire going, so he sat before it to warm himself.

"How was the oak?" asked his wife.

The woodcutter didn't want to admit that he hadn't chopped down the oak tree, so he told his wife that he'd found some better trees on the way there. He quickly changed the subject.

"All that chopping and icy-cold air has made me hungry, wife," he said. "I wish I had a nice string of sausages to eat!"

No sooner had he said it than a string of sausages fell down the chimney and dropped straight into the roaring fire, where they started to sizzle away and smell quite delicious.

The woodcutter's wife leapt up and shouted, "What's all this?"

The woodcutter realized that the fairy hadn't been a dream after all, so he told his wife the whole story.

As he told it, his wife got redder in the face until she looked fit to burst. "Why, you great lumbering fool!" she exclaimed. "A fairy grants you three wishes and you waste one of them on sausages? What a silly thing to do!"

The wife moaned and complained at the woodcutter until he couldn't bear it and, without thinking, he cried, "Good wife! Please will you stop going on about sausages? Why, I wish they were stuck up your nose! That would keep you quiet!"

In an instant, his second wish came true and the string of sausages was dangling from the end of his poor wife's nose!

The woodcutter gasped at what he had done, and his wife shrieked at the sight of the sausages hanging down before her. Together, they tried to pull them out of her nose, but they were stuck fast!

There was just one wish left, and only one thing that could be done with it. The woodcutter wished that the sausages weren't up his wife's nose.

Though he had wasted his three wishes on silly things rather than the riches he had always dreamt of, that evening, he and his wife shared the best plate of sausages they had ever eaten!

Sleeping Beauty

Once upon a time, a king and queen longed for a daughter with all their hearts. When at last the queen gave birth to a beautiful baby girl, everyone celebrated.

The king was so overjoyed that he decided to host a great banquet—the grandest there had ever been. He invited all the fairies in the land, except for one. She was a miserable old crone who hadn't been seen for so long, everyone thought she had died.

The banquet was a huge success and a splendid time was had by all. Everyone thought the new princess was the sweetest baby they had ever seen.

❧☙

As the night drew to a close, the twelve fairies stepped forward to present the little princess with some special gifts, as was their custom. The first fairy gave her the gift of courage, the second gave her intelligence, the third gave her kindness, and so on, until the newborn was blessed with many of the most desirable virtues. But just as the twelfth fairy was about to present her gift, the thirteenth fairy —the mean old crone—stormed into the hall in a terrible rage.

"How dare you not invite me!" she screeched at the king and queen. "My gift to your daughter is a curse—when she has turned fifteen, she will prick her finger on a spindle and die!"

The thirteenth fairy disappeared in a cloud of thick black smoke and the entire court gasped with horror. The queen turned ghostly pale with fright.

However, there was still hope, as the twelfth fairy had not yet granted her gift. "With my powers, I can make sure that the princess doesn't die," she said. "Instead, she will fall into a deep sleep that lasts for one hundred years and will be broken by true love's kiss."

The next morning, the king and queen issued a decree that every spindle in the kingdom should be burnt. They hoped that this would put an end to the terrible curse that hung over their beloved daughter.

In time, people even forgot about the curse—and the princess grew up to be every bit as brave, kind-hearted, talented, and charming, as you would expect a girl blessed by fairies to be.

But, one day, just after she had turned fifteen, her curiosity got the better of her and, while exploring the castle, she found a spiral staircase she had never seen before. It led to a small room at the top of a turret.

Inside the room, there was an old lady, spinning flax on a spindle. She was really the cruel thirteenth fairy in disguise! The princess had never seen a spindle before and was eager to try her hand at spinning, but, as soon as she touched the spindle, she pricked her finger and immediately slumped to the floor in a deep sleep.

The wicked fairy disappeared at once, and, as she did so, she used her cruel magic to spread her curse across the whole palace.

The king, who had just returned from a hunt, fell asleep next to his horse in the stable—and all the horses in the stable fell asleep too. The queen fell asleep while sitting on her throne. The cook in the kitchen dropped the chicken she had been plucking and started to snore. A maid dropped the dishes she was washing and fell into a slumber. The dogs in the courtyard and even the doves on the roof all fell asleep too.

"One by one, every living thing

...in the castle fell into a deep and dreamless sleep."

As the years passed, a tall, thorny hedge grew up around the castle, so that you could only just see its highest turret poking out above it.

Occasionally, daring adventurers, who had heard tales of a beautiful princess trapped inside a lost castle in a hundred-year sleep, would attempt to hack their way through the thorns—but they didn't get far.

At last, when the hundred years were almost over, a prince was journeying through the kingdom and stopped at a local inn for refreshments. Over lunch, the innkeeper told him the legend of the cursed princess.

"Only a fool would dare to enter the forest, for the thorns will trap them there forever!" said the innkeeper.

"I'm not afraid," said the prince—who loved a challenge—and he set off in the direction of the hidden castle, determined to save the mysterious princess from her endless slumber.

When he reached the edge of the thorny forest, he drew his sword to cut his way through and was surprised to see the thorns turn into wild roses, and the tangled branches separate to clear a path before him.

He walked through the forest to the castle and was amazed by the strange sight before him—everyone from the stable boys to the king himself was fast asleep.

He walked past the sleeping queen on the throne, his footsteps echoing loudly in the silence, and at last, he found the princess, who truly was a Sleeping Beauty.

In fact, the prince found himself so in awe, he couldn't help but kiss her. In that very moment when his lips touched hers, Sleeping Beauty opened her eyes—as did the king, the queen, the cook, the maids, the horses, the dogs, and the doves.

Indeed, everyone in the castle sprang suddenly to life and every room was filled with noisy laughter and chatter, as people stretched and yawned and wondered how on earth they had ended up on the floor.

The prince took Sleeping Beauty by the hand and led her to the throne room, where she was reunited with her mother and father—and they all lived happily ever after.

The Snow Queen

Once upon a time, there was a wicked hobgoblin who made a magic mirror. The magic mirror made anything that was beautiful or kind look ugly and mean, and it put misery in the hearts of anyone who looked at it.

One day, the mirror smashed into a million tiny pieces and scattered all over the world. Some pieces flew into people's eyes, which made them see the bad in everything, and some flew into people's hearts, freezing them to ice.

Far from where the mirror smashed, there lived a little boy called Kay and a little girl called Gerda. They were best friends and often played together on the balcony that joined their apartments. Their parents had planted beautiful roses there, and the children loved to play among them.

They were playing one day when two tiny splinters of the hobgoblin's mirror came flying through the air. One flew into Kay's eye and the other sliced into his heart. Kay felt pain for a few seconds, but his personality changed instantly. He was cold and unkind to Gerda and no longer wanted to play— her poor little heart felt broken.

Soon, winter came and a thick dusting of snow turned everything white. Kay abandoned Gerda to go sledding in the town square. After a while, a splendid carriage appeared with a driver wrapped in a white fur cloak.

Feeling bold, Kay tied his sled to the back of the carriage so that he could sleigh faster. The driver turned and nodded at Kay, then sped out through the town gates with Kay trailing behind. Kay shouted at the driver to stop, but the wind howled around him and drowned out his cries.

They journeyed for many miles until, in the middle of nowhere, the carriage came to an abrupt halt. Shivering with cold and fear, Kay saw the driver step down and discovered that she was a lady, dressed all in sparkling white. She was the Snow Queen.

"Here, climb into my carriage and creep into my warm furs," she told Kay. The Snow Queen kissed Kay's forehead and, though at first it felt like an icy dagger, he soon forgot the cold completely. She drove the carriage on, up through the wintry sky and across the clouds.

At last, they came to a magnificent

palace carved from a glacier of ice.

When Kay didn't return that day, nobody knew what had become of him. Many tears were shed, and little Gerda sobbed hardest of all. People thought he must be dead, but Gerda refused to believe it. When spring came, she decided to search for her lost friend. She walked down to the river and stepped into a small boat. The current quickly swept her along and deep into the countryside.

Eventually, she came to a cherry orchard with a sweet little house in the middle. It had a thatched roof and a wonderful flower garden. An old woman came out of the house, wearing a big sun hat with glorious flowers painted on it.

"You poor child!" the old woman exclaimed. "However did you drift so far into the great wide world?" The old woman lifted Gerda out of the boat.

Gerda told the old woman all about her friend Kay and asked if she had seen him. The old woman said that he might be along soon, and she offered Gerda some cherries. Now, the old woman wasn't a witch, but she was magic—and she had always wanted a little girl of her own.

While Gerda ate the sweet cherries, the old woman combed her blonde ringlets until the little girl quite forgot about her friend.

The next day and for many weeks after that, Gerda played in the old woman's garden. She was very happy until, one day, she saw the roses painted on the old woman's hat.

Suddenly, all her memories of playing on the balcony with Kay came flooding back to her. She ran down the garden path and through the gate, leaving the magical old woman behind.

Out in the world, it was turning to winter again and the frost was starting to nip. Gerda soon grew cold and tired. She stopped to rest for a while and was joined by a big black crow.

"Where are you going in the great wide world?" he asked. Gerda told the crow the story of her missing friend Kay and asked if he had seen him.

The crow nodded his head and cawed, "Maybe I have, maybe I have!" Then he told Gerda how a boy like Kay had just married the Princess. "My lady love has the run of the palace," he said proudly. "I heard it straight from her!"

"Oh, I must see him!" cried Gerda, and the crow agreed to help her. He led Gerda to a secret staircase at the palace. As she walked up the stairs, her heart pounded with excitement at the thought of seeing Kay again. The crow's lady love met her at the top—she was a female crow with kind, twinkly eyes.

"I shall lead the way," she cawed softly.

Soon, the two entered the royal bedroom, where two grand beds hung from the ceiling. One bed was white and in it lay the sleeping Princess. Gerda crept to the other bed and gently called out Kay's name, but when the startled Prince sat up, she saw that he wasn't her friend Kay at all.

Gerda sobbed with disappointment and told the Prince and Princess her story.

"Poor little thing," they said kindly and they gave Gerda a warm bed for the night. The next day, the royal couple invited Gerda to stay, but instead she asked them for a little carriage, so she could continue her search for Kay.

The Prince and Princess agreed to help and they gave Gerda a carriage of pure gold with her own horse and coachman. She thanked them for their kindness and waved goodbye.

Sadly, Gerda hadn't gone far when her carriage was attacked by a ruthless band of robbers. They dragged Gerda onto the dusty road and threatened her, but the daughter of one of the robbers wanted a playmate, so Gerda's life was spared.

Back at their hideout, the robber girl showed Gerda her room and the animals she kept imprisoned there—hundreds of wood pigeons were trapped in cages and there was a frightened-looking reindeer. Gerda felt so sorry for them.

The girl mistook Gerda for a princess, but Gerda told her all about her lost friend, Kay, and her journey to find him. Though the robber girl liked Gerda, at bedtime, she still clasped an arm around her neck so her new playmate couldn't escape.

Poor Gerda was so scared she couldn't fall asleep. Then, suddenly, in the darkness, she heard the wood pigeons say, "Coo, coo! We have seen Kay in the Snow Queen's sleigh. They swooped over our nest. Coo, coo!"

"Where were they going?" whispered Gerda.

"Her stronghold is a castle near the North Pole," said the reindeer.

In the morning, Gerda told the robber girl what the animals had said in the night. The robber girl thought Gerda was very brave, so she decided to help her.

She gave Gerda her mother's fur mittens to keep her hands warm and untied the reindeer. "Reindeer, carry this little girl to the Snow Queen's palace," she said. "Go quickly, before the robbers awake!" The robber girl wished them good luck.

With Gerda on his back, the reindeer bounded away, straight through the great forest and across the plains, as fast as he could run. All night long, the skies flashed with the magical Northern Lights.

At last, looking for shelter, they came to a small hut. Inside it was a Finnish woman. The reindeer told her Gerda's story, while Gerda warmed herself by the fire.

"Won't you give the girl something magical to drink, so that she may overpower the Snow Queen?" he asked.

"Much good that would do!" the Finn woman sniffed. "Kay is indeed with the Snow Queen, and he loves it because of the splinters of mirror in his heart and in his eye. As long as they are there, he is in her power. No potion I can make is as great as the power Gerda has in her heart. Don't you see how humans and beasts help her, and how far she has come? You must carry her to the Snow Queen's palace!"

The Finn woman lifted Gerda onto the reindeer, and he galloped as fast as he could until they came to the garden of the icy palace. Here, he set Gerda down.

There was not a cloud in the sky, yet the snowflakes swirled around Gerda, getting thicker and faster. She tried to run through them, but they grew larger and formed sharp, ugly shapes—like icy monsters. These were the Snow Queen's guards.

It was so cold that Gerda's breath froze in the air and took on the shape of little angels, who dropped to the ground and fought off the Snow Queen's icy monsters, shattering them into tiny pieces.

Gerda bravely stepped into the Snow Queen's palace, where the walls were ice and the windows were the knife-edged wind. The halls were lit by the Northern Lights and in the middle of the largest hall was a frozen lake, where the Snow Queen sat when she was at home. But today she had flown south so, instead, Kay sat there all alone, looking stiff and blue with cold.

Gerda threw her arms around him and cried, "Dearest Kay! I've found you at last!" But Kay was as still as a statue.

Gerda cried hot tears, and when they fell on him, they went straight into his heart, burning away the splinter of mirror that was lodged there. Then Kay burst into tears too, and the piece of mirror in his eye was washed right out.

He cried with happiness, "Gerda! Where have you been?" Then he looked around him and said, "And where have I been? How cold it is here!"

He hugged Gerda, who kissed his cheeks to turn them pink. When Kay felt warm again, they strolled, hand in hand, out of the icy prison to find the reindeer waiting for them. Clinging tightly to each other, the two friends rode all the way home.

Kay and Gerda were just in time to see the first buds of spring, and when they walked into their homes, everything was just as they had left it. The roses on the balcony were in full bloom, so Kay and Gerda sat beneath them, and the icy sadness of the Snow Queen's palace soon felt like a distant dream.

Thumbelina

By Hans Christian Andersen

Once upon a time, there was a woman who wanted a child but couldn't have one, so she decided to ask the fairies for help.

The fairy queen gave her a small seed and said, "Plant this in a flower pot and good luck will come your way."

The woman thanked the fairy queen and, in just a few days, a beautiful red tulip grew in the pot.

"What a pretty flower!" said the woman and she bent down to take a closer look. As she did so, the tulip petals opened up to reveal a tiny girl, no bigger than your thumb.

The woman lifted the sweet little child, who was as light as a feather. The woman smiled and said, "I will call you Thumbelina!"

That night, the woman nestled the girl in a bed made from a walnut shell lined with small petals, with a velvety red rose petal for a blanket.

The next morning, to amuse her tiny child, the woman placed a large dish on the table, filled with water and leaves. Thumbelina used the leaves as boats and paddled from side to side. In the afternoon, the woman told Thumbelina stories and taught her how to read and write. Later that day, the little girl sang songs with a voice as sweet as a fairy's.

And so it went for many months. The woman and her teeny child were blissfully happy together.

However, one day, the woman was busy in the garden and Thumbelina was drawing a picture, when a large toad crept out from behind a rock.

"That fair maiden would make a fine wife for my son," thought the toad, and she crawled over to Thumbelina and grabbed her. Little Thumbelina cried out, but her mother didn't hear her.

When they reached the stream where the toad lived, she called her son, who saw pretty little Thumbelina and said, "Croak, croak."

Thumbelina cowered to see such an ugly beast.

"Don't frighten your new wife!" said the toad's mother. "I will put her on a lily pad in the middle of the stream, so she can't escape, and we'll prepare for your wedding."

The mother toad carried Thumbelina to the lily pad and left her there. All alone, Thumbelina sat and wept.

Soon, her crying was heard by the fish who lived there. They popped their heads out of the water and Thumbelina told them her plight.

"A dainty girl like you can't marry a big toad!" they said and, together, the fish nibbled at the lily pad's stem until it broke free and floated down the stream, far away from the toads.

"Good luck, Thumbelina!" cried the fish, and she waved to them as the lily pad carried her away.

On and on the stream flowed, passing through villages and towns. The sun danced on the river, making it look like liquid gold. At last, a beautiful butterfly landed on the lily pad next to her.

"What a delicate little thing you are," said the butterfly, and Thumbelina curtseyed to him gracefully. "Tie a ribbon around my back to hold on to and I'll take you for a ride!"

The butterfly took off and Thumbelina clung tightly to its back, admiring the view of flower-filled fields below.

But, suddenly, a large, clumsy beetle flew by and bumped into the butterfly, knocking Thumbelina off.

Thumbelina fell to the ground, landing in the centre of a daisy on the edge of a forest. For the rest of the summer, she made the forest her home. She wove a hammock from blades of grass and hung it under a big leaf for shelter. She drank dew and sipped nectar from flowers. She sang with the birds and made a good life for herself. But when winter came, and the birds flew away and the flowers wilted, she soon grew lonely, hungry, and cold. Certain she would starve, Thumbelina left the forest in search of a new home.

At last, hidden in a hedgerow across a field, she found a little red door.

When she tapped at it, it was opened by a friendly field mouse.

"Poor girl!" cried the mouse, when he saw how cold she looked. "Do come in and warm yourself by the fire." He shared his food with her, as she told him her sorry tale.

"You are welcome to stay with me," he said. "All I ask is that you keep my home tidy—and tell me some stories."

Thumbelina was most grateful for the mouse's kindness—and she kept his house sparkling clean.

Soon, they had a visit from a mole in a smart velvet coat. As he entered, the mouse whispered to Thumbelina:

'Be sure to tell him your best stories,

for he loves to hear a tale or two."

So Thumbelina told the mole about the singing birds and the golden sun on the river. She told him of dainty butterflies and beautiful flowers—but the mole wasn't interested. He thought his underground world was far more entertaining. However, he fell in love with Thumbelina's sweet voice and started to visit more often.

One day, he invited the field mouse and Thumbelina to walk with him in a new tunnel he had built. As they walked along the gloomy passage, they found a dead swallow. It had fallen through a hole in the tunnel and looked like it had died of cold.

The mole pushed it to one side and said, "How miserable to be a bird. All they do is tweet all day until winter kills them."

But Thumbelina's heart ached to see the little bird lying there. The mole and field mouse walked on, and she stayed with the swallow. "Perhaps it was you who sang with me in the forest," she said.

She gathered some hay and draped it over the swallow like a blanket and, as she did so, she heard the very faint beating of its heart.

"You're alive!" smiled Thumbelina. She stayed with the bird all night and, by morning, it had opened its eyes.

"Thank you so much, little maiden—you have saved my life. I will soon be able to fly again," said the swallow.

Over the next few weeks, Thumbelina secretly nursed the swallow back to health. When it was strong enough to fly again, it said, "Will you come with me? I think you will like my home."

"I can't," said Thumbelina sadly, as she didn't want to hurt the feelings of the field mouse, who had been so kind to her. Instead, she watched the swallow fly through the tunnel and out into the spring sunshine.

Later that day, the mouse scurried home, chattering with excitement. "I have wonderful news, Thumbelina! The mole wants to marry you! He is a fine gentlemen with cellars full of food—you are very lucky indeed."

But Thumbelina didn't feel lucky—she didn't want to marry the mole. However, the field mouse didn't hear her pleas—he was too busy making her wedding gown, while she stared out of the window, wishing she had flown off with the swallow when she had the chance.

On her wedding day, Thumbelina decided to go outside one last time. As she stood in the field, she shouted, "Goodbye, blue sky! Farewell, flowers! Say hello to the swallow for me!"

Suddenly, she heard a familiar "Tweet, Tweet," and there was her swallow friend. He swooped down beside her and she told him of her awful fate.

"Come with me, Thumbelina. We can fly far from here to a place where the sun always shines. You saved my life and now I can save yours!"

Thumbelina didn't waste a moment. She climbed onto the swallow's back and off they soared, over forest and sea and mountain and valley. Tiny Thumbelina couldn't believe the wonderful sights she could see.

At last, they reached a crystal blue lake, surrounded by lush green trees. There was a marble palace next to it, and the swallow's nest was in the eaves of the palace roof.

"This is my home," said the swallow, "but this is not comfortable for you."

So he flew down to some beautiful flowers in the gardens below and placed her gently on a petal. When Thumbelina climbed into the middle of the flower, she gasped to see a tiny man there, with a golden crown and two gossamer wings. He was only a little taller than Thumbelina and he was incredibly handsome.

He told Thumbelina that he was the king of the flowers and, when he heard her story, he was so enchanted by her, he asked Thumbelina to marry him.

"Yes!" laughed Thumbelina, and all the flowers around them opened up. From each one came a flower fairy with a gift for Thumbelina. All the gifts were splendid, but the best was a pair of fairy wings, so that she too could flutter from flower to flower.

And that is how a tiny girl—no bigger than your thumb—became the fairy queen of flowers.

Rumpelstiltskin

Once upon a time, there was a poor miller who lived alone with his only daughter, Sabine.

One day, when the king was returning from a hunt, he stopped at the miller's cottage to ask for a cool drink. Desperate to impress the king, the miller told him a terrible lie—he said that Sabine had the power to spin straw into gold. The king was a terribly greedy man, so his eyes lit up at such news.

"Is that so?" said the king. "If your daughter is as gifted as you claim she is, send her to my castle tomorrow and I will put her to the test."

When Sabine heard her father's lie, she was furious with him, but she didn't want to get him into trouble with the king so, the next day, she presented herself at the castle.

The king greeted her, and showed her to a room that was stacked high with straw. In the corner stood a spinning wheel and a small stool.

"Now get to work," said the king, rubbing his hands together greedily. "And if I find any straw here tomorrow morning, your father will be punished!"

The king locked the door behind him, leaving Sabine in great despair. What was she to do? She had no idea how to spin straw into gold! As the night wore on, Sabine grew so frightened of what the king would do, she burst into tears.

But at the stroke of midnight, the door opened and in walked an odd little man. He was no taller than Sabine's waist and he had a long beard that reached the floor. He wore a red pointed hat and red shoes to match.

"Dear girl," he said. "What is making you cry like this?"

"I have to spin this straw into gold for the king," Sabine sobbed, "and I don't know how!"

"I know how!" said the little man. "What will you give me if I spin it for you?"

"You can have my necklace," said Sabine, and she offered it to him.

The little man took her necklace and sat down at the spinning wheel. He whirred away and, in no time at all, he had spun a reel of gold from straw.

In no time at all, he had spun a reel of gold from straw

The little man carried on spinning and, soon enough, all the straw had gone and the room glittered with reels of gold. Sabine couldn't believe it!

After he had gone, she fell asleep on the floor and was woken at dawn by the king, who was delighted to see that the miller had been telling the truth—Sabine really could turn straw into gold! But the sight of all that gold just made the king greedier.

That afternoon, he took Sabine to an even bigger room, stacked even higher with straw. He commanded her to spin the straw into gold by the morning or face a cruel punishment.

Once again, Sabine wept with despair and, once again, at midnight, the odd little man entered the room.

"What will you give me this time if I spin the straw for you?" he asked.

"You can have my ring," said Sabine.

He took the ring and, just as before, he sat at the wheel and spun the straw into gold with great ease.

The king came early the next morning and he was overjoyed by the gold, but he wasn't satisfied. He led Sabine to an even larger room, which was stacked to the ceiling with straw.

"Spin this into gold by the morning and I will make you my son's wife," said the king. "Do not fail me!"

Now Sabine had two worries—she still couldn't spin straw into gold, and she had nothing left to give the odd little man if he appeared again. But when he arrived at midnight, he already knew what he wanted.

"I will spin this straw for you," he said craftily, "if you give me your first child when you become queen."

"Well," thought Sabine, "I doubt the king will truly allow me to marry the prince, so I will never be queen." And she agreed to the little man's request. In return, he spun the straw into towering piles of golden reels.

When the king returned at dawn, his greed was finally satisfied and, much to Sabine's surprise, he kept his promise to her.

Sabine and the prince were married, and they made a very happy couple (for, luckily, the prince was not at all like his father). Within a year, they had a beautiful baby boy.

Sadly, soon after their child was born, the king died and, overnight, the prince became king and Sabine was his queen.

A few days later, Queen Sabine was in her chambers when the odd little man suddenly appeared before her. She had forgotten all about the deal she had made with him.

"It is time to fulfil your half of the bargain, Queen," said the little man, pointing at her son in his cradle.

Sabine was horrified, and offered him all the riches in her kingdom if he would only let her keep her child. He refused, but she wept so much that he began to feel pity for her.

"I will make another deal with you," said the little man. "I will visit you for the next three nights and, if you can guess my name in that time, you can keep your child. If not, he is mine."

The queen was forced to agree and she spent the rest of that night and the following day thinking up names that might suit her strange visitor.

When the little man appeared the following evening, the queen had a long list of names before her.

She read them out, but the little man just shook his head. She ended with, "Ludwig, Conrad, Bob?"

"That's not my name!" laughed the little man. "You have two more chances!" And he skipped out of her chamber with a wide grin on his face.

The next day, Queen Sabine sent messengers to every village and town in the kingdom to collect names. That night, her list was far longer, but as she read out the names, the little man shook his head again and chuckled.

Desperate, Sabine turned to some of the more unusual names on the list,

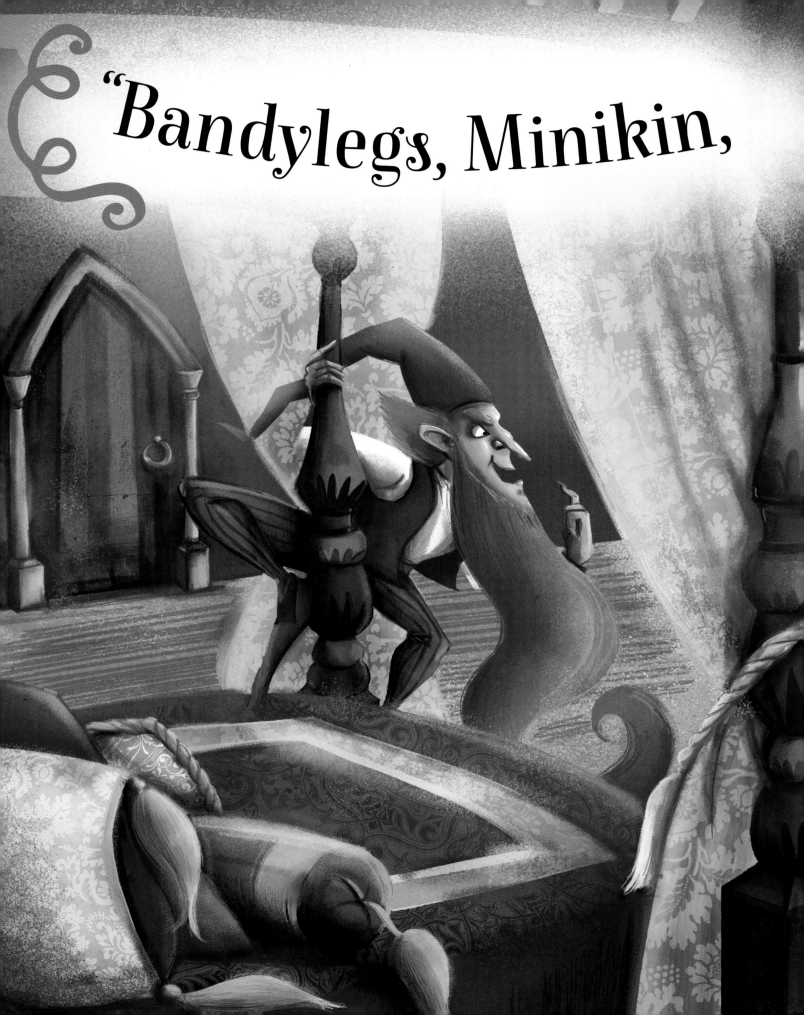

"Bandylegs, Minikin,

Redtop?"

"No! That's not my name!" he laughed. "One more chance left for you!" And he skipped gleefully through the door.

The next day, Queen Sabine sent her royal messengers deep into the woods and high into the mountains to collect more names. They returned later that day with only one new name for her list.

"Dear Queen," said one of the messengers. "High in the mountains, I came across a small wooden hut. When I looked through the window, I saw an odd little man jigging around and singing a song that went like this:

'Today I jig, tomorrow I'll go
To fetch the queen's young babe,
I'm so clever, nobody knows
Rumpelstiltskin is my name!'"

The queen was thrilled to hear the messenger's good news and it had come just at the right time—a few minutes later, the odd little man appeared again.

"Your last chance, mistress Queen! Can you guess my name?"

"Is it Franz?" said the queen.

"That's not my name!" grinned the little man, and he jumped up and down excitedly.

"Hmmm... Hubert?" asked the queen.

"No! That's not my name!" the little man squealed and he broke into a jig.

"Oh dear," said the queen. "What about... hmmm... Rumpelstiltskin?"

The little man stopped dancing. He stood with his mouth gaping open. "How... how did you guess?"

Then he grew red with rage and stomped his feet hard on the castle's stone floor. He jumped up and down so hard, in fact, that he made a huge hole in the floor and plunged deep into the chasm below.

The last Queen Sabine saw of him was the pointed tip of his red hat disappearing down the hole—and that was the end of Rumpelstiltskin!

From that day on, Queen Sabine, the king, their baby, and the miller all lived together in peace and harmony.

Hansel and Gretel

Once upon a time, there lived a poor woodcutter, with his two sweet children—Hansel and Gretel—and their new stepmother.

They had barely a crust to eat between them and, one night, long after the two children had gone to bed, the worried woodcutter said to his wife, "There isn't enough here to feed the children. What shall we do?"

"I have an idea," said his wife. "Let's take the children deep into the woods tomorrow morning. We can make a fire for them and leave them there. That way, we'll have two less mouths to feed!"

The woodcutter was horrified by his wife's idea. "Abandon my own children!" he cried. "How could you suggest such a terrible thing?"

"Then we'll starve!" she shouted. And she nagged him until he agreed to her plan.

But her shouting woke Hansel and Gretel and they heard every word she said. Gretel's little heart was broken, but Hansel said, "Don't worry, sister. I have an idea."

And when the grown-ups fell asleep, he crept out of the house into the moonlight and picked up a pocketful of shiny white pebbles.

Before dawn had broken the next morning, their stepmother shook the two children awake.

"Get up, you lazy pair! We are going to help your father today."

She gave them each a dry crust of bread and said, "Don't eat it too soon, as it's all we have." Then they set off together for the woods.

After a little while, Hansel stopped and looked back at their house. He kept doing this every few minutes.

"Why do you keep stopping, boy?" cried their stepmother, impatiently.

"I thought I saw a white cat on our roof, so I was waving goodbye to it!" said Hansel.

"Oh, you foolish boy!" sighed his stepmother. "That's no cat—it's just the sun shining on the roof tiles."

But Hansel hadn't really seen a cat. He was dropping a trail of shiny white pebbles along the path. As they walked deeper into the woods, Hansel carefully dropped more pebbles behind him.

When they woke up, the fire had dwindled and it was getting dark. A tear rolled down Gretel's cheek.

"I hoped that Father would come back for us," she said sadly. "How will we ever find our way home?"

Hansel took his sister's hand and said, "Just wait until the moon rises—then we will be safe."

And, sure enough, when the moon rose, Hansel spotted a white pebble shining in the moonlight.

"Follow me," smiled Hansel, and he led his sister through the woods, following his trail of shiny white pebbles.

When they reached home, Hansel and Gretel knocked on the door and their stepmother answered. She was shocked to see them, but their father pushed her aside and hugged them. He was happier than ever to see them.

A few weeks passed by and the woodcutter's family ran out of food again. His wife began to shout at him and nag him to leave the children in the woods again and he soon felt forced to give in.

At last they reached a clearing, where their father had made a fire for them.

"This will keep you warm," he said. Then, with a sad face, he kissed his children goodbye.

"Now wait here!" said their stepmother, sternly. "We will fetch you when we have finished."

Hansel and Gretel sat by the fire and waited. At lunchtime, they ate their bread and then, by the warmth of the fire, they drifted off to sleep.

As before, Hansel and Gretel heard every word, so when their parents fell asleep, Hansel crept out of bed to fill his pockets with pebbles. But, this time, their stepmother had locked the front door.

"Don't worry, Gretel. I will think of something," said Hansel.

Before dawn, their stepmother shook the children awake. "Here," she said, thrusting thin crusts into their hands. "We are going into the woods and that is all the food we have, so don't eat it all at once!"

They set off for the woods, but Hansel kept stopping and looking back.

"Why do you keep stopping, boy?" snapped his stepmother.

"I thought I saw a white pigeon on our roof, so I was waving goodbye to it!"

"Oh, you foolish boy!" cried his stepmother. "That's no pigeon—it's just the sun shining on the roof tiles."

But Hansel hadn't really seen a pigeon. He was breaking up the bread crust in his pocket and dropping a secret trail of crumbs behind him. He did this all the way into the deep, dark woods.

When they reached the clearing where their father had made a big fire, their stepmother said, "Wait here and we will fetch you when we have finished."

The children waited patiently and Gretel shared her bread with Hansel. Soon, they fell asleep and, when they woke up, it was nighttime.

"Just wait for the moon, sister," said Hansel, "and we can follow the bread crumbs home again."

But when the moon rose, there was not a crumb in sight, because the woodland birds had eaten them all. Hansel and Gretel wandered through the woods looking for the path, but without the crumbs, they got lost.

The children walked all night and all the next day until their tummies rumbled and their feet ached. Just when they thought they could walk no more, they stumbled into a clearing with a sweet little house in it.

It was made from gingerbread
and it tasted delicious!

The house smelled wonderful and the two children were so hungry, they ran up the path and broke off big chunks of gingerbread to eat. It was the most delicious thing they had ever tasted.

As they nibbled away, a frail old lady hobbled out of the house, hunched over her walking stick. Hansel and Gretel dropped their food in fright.

"Oh, you poor things!" she said. "You look so hungry. Don't you worry now, I'll take good care of you." And she invited them inside, where she treated them to sweet pancakes and milk.

When the children were full, the old lady made up two comfortable beds for them to sleep in and, that night, Hansel and Gretel slept peacefully.

The children didn't know that the old lady was really a wicked witch and she liked to eat rosy-cheeked little children! The witch had poor eyesight, but an excellent sense of smell and, when she had picked up the scent of Hansel and Gretel in the woods, she had put an enchantment on her house to tempt them inside.

The next morning, the witch wrapped her bony fingers around Hansel's wrist, dragged him from his bed and locked him in a cage in her kitchen.

Gretel cried out, but the witch just screeched, "Stop whining! Now cook something good for your brother. I want to fatten him up and eat him!"

That day and for many days afterwards, poor Gretel was forced to cook huge meals to fatten up her brother—and, every night, the witch hobbled over to Hansel's cage and said, "Hold out your hand. Let me feel how fat you are getting."

But Hansel was clever and he held out a chicken bone instead. The old witch's eyesight was so bad that she felt the bone and wondered why Hansel wasn't getting any plumper.

After a few weeks, the witch got tired of waiting for Hansel to grow plump. "Gretel!" she cackled. "Light the oven. I am going to eat your brother today!"

Gretel wept to hear the news, but she did as she was told. The witch stood by her and screeched, "Gretel, lean inside the oven and check if the fire is hot enough!"

But Gretel knew what the witch was up to, so she said, "I don't know how!"

"Silly child!" snapped the old witch, and she leaned inside the oven to show Gretel how to do it.

Wasting no time, Gretel leapt forward and pushed the witch into the oven's roaring flames, slamming the door behind her!

Gretel then dashed over to Hansel and freed him from his cage, and the brother and sister jumped for joy!

Before they left the witch's house, they filled their pockets with precious stones and coins, then they made their way into the woods, hoping to find home.

They walked for a whole day and night until, at last, the woods started to look more familiar. Before long, they found a path they recognized, and it led them right to their house!

Their father was overjoyed to see them again and he wrapped his arms around them tightly. In the time they had been gone, their stepmother had died, and their father had searched the woods each day to find his children.

The clever pair ran to the kitchen table and emptied their pockets of the witch's gems and coins. With their stepmother gone and so many riches, Hansel, Gretel, and their father were able to live without a worry in the world.

The Golden Staff

Long ago, at the dawn of time, the most powerful god of all, Viracocha, fashioned the first people of South America from clay.

Though he gave them voices and crops to harvest, the people had no skills—they didn't know how to make clothes or build houses. They couldn't read or write or cook—so, for a long time, they lived like animals.

The sun god, Inti, looked down on the people and he felt pity for them, so he decided that the cleverest of his four sons and his daughter should rule over everyone and teach them how to live in a better way. Their names were Manco Cápac and Mama Ocllo.

"Teach them how to live together in harmony and help them to build a great civilization," he told his children. "Be a father and mother to them all."

And he handed them a magical golden staff that shone like the sun.

"On your travels, you will find a place where this golden staff sinks deep into the ground with just one blow. There, you must build a great city—this place will be the heart of your empire and home to a magnificent sun temple, where the people can come and worship me," said Inti.

As the sun rose the next morning, Inti took Manco Cápac and Mama Ocllo to the Isla del Sol, an island in the centre of Lake Titicaca in Bolivia, where he was born. "Begin your journey here, my children."

However, Manco Cápac and Mama Ocllo didn't realize that their three brothers were deeply jealous of the important task they had been given, and they wanted to rule the new empire all by themselves. Just as Manco Cápac and Mama Ocllo set out on their journey, the brothers stepped out of a nearby cave.

Manco Cápac and Mama Ocllo thought that their siblings had come to help them, so they greeted their brothers warmly and set out together to teach the people. But they hadn't gone far when one of their brothers, Ayar Cachi, made fun of the humans.

"What idiots!" he sneered. "Look at them. Who would want to teach such dumb beasts? What a waste of my powers! I can knock down hills with a single shot of my sling—and that's far more fun than hanging around with these fools!" And Ayar Cachi destroyed a hill with his slingshot, injuring the people who lived there.

Manco Cápac was so angered by his brother's foolishness and destruction, he used his powers to send Ayar Cachi back to the cave where he came from, and sealed him inside.

On seeing this, the second brother, Ayar Uchu, grew fearful of Manco Cápac's strength. "Perhaps I will go back to the cave and look after the people from there." And he ran back to the cave as quickly as he could. When Inti, the sun god, saw this, he turned Ayar Uchu into stone to punish him for his cowardice.

The third brother, Ayar Auca, was, by now, quaking with fear. He ran off into the forest and was never seen again!

And so, as Inti first intended, only Manco Cápac and Mama Ocllo remained. The brother and sister journeyed far and wide, uniting many different tribes of people, teaching them how to build their own homes and villages, how to farm and weave and cook, and how to read and write.

A great civilization grew around them and the people loved their leaders, Manco Cápac and Mama Ocllo.

After many years of teaching, they reached a place called Cusco in a river valley in Peru. Here, as in many places before, Manco Cápac tried to drive the golden staff into the soil and found that, at last, it sank into the ground with great ease.

In an instant, a stunning temple to the sun god, Inti, sprang up before them —it had walls of glittering gold and a courtyard filled with golden statues.

Inside, there was a golden wall with a spectacular carving of the sun, which lit up the whole temple. They called the temple the Sun House.

With Inti's temple in place, Manco Cápac and Mama Ocllo set to work building a great city around it and a palace for themselves. From there, they ruled over the city they had created and all the people around it—and that is how the Incan empire came to be.

The Little Mermaid

By Hans Christian Andersen

Once upon a time, there lived a Sea King in a spectacular coral palace at the bottom of the ocean. He lived with his six mermaid daughters.

Of his six daughters, the youngest was the quietest. While her sisters played, she tended to the special garden she had planted, which was filled with beautiful sea flowers. Her most treasured part of the garden was a statue of a man she had found in a shipwreck. She would sit by the statue for many hours, dreaming of the world above the sea and what it might be like to be human.

Sometimes, her grandmother would tell her tales of the places she had seen in her youth—tales of animals, magnificent buildings, and fragrant blooms; bathing on warm beaches in the moonlight, and listening to human voices in the distance.

"I wish I could see it," sighed the little mermaid, and her grandmother would always give the same answer: "Soon enough, my dear, soon enough."

It was true—in a few years, on her fifteenth birthday, the little mermaid would finally be allowed to swim above the surface of the sea.

The years passed and the little mermaid watched with envy as her sisters each turned fifteen and were allowed to see the human world. They always returned with wide smiles and sparkling eyes.

"How was it? Is it beautiful? Did you see a human?" asked the mermaid, but her sisters just answered: "Soon enough, my dear, soon enough."

The little mermaid thought she might explode with curiosity!

At last, the day came when the little mermaid turned fifteen. She could barely wait to swim above the waves, but her grandmother took her to one side. "You deserve to look special today, my dear." And she placed a stunning pearl tiara on the excited mermaid's head. "Now off you go!"

The little mermaid soared eagerly to the surface and, when she finally saw the world above, she was astounded by its beauty. The sun was setting over a calm sea, turning everything vivid orange and hot pink. The clouds in the sky seemed to be lined with gold and, not too far away, there was a splendid ship, its sails fluttering in the breeze.

"The world is more beautiful than I ever

imagined!" smiled the little mermaid.

She heard music drifting across the water and swam closer the ship to get a better look. As she drew nearer, she saw that it was decorated with bunting and lanterns.

She spied through a window a ballroom filled with smartly dressed people, all dancing, laughing, and talking. They were celebrating the sixteenth birthday of a young prince.

When the little mermaid caught sight of the prince, she was enchanted and couldn't take her eyes away. She stayed for many hours watching him, as he smiled and talked to his guests.

It was very late when the sea became restless. Most of the guests had gone to bed, but the prince was still on the deck, gazing at the stars.

The sea began to churn and gloomy clouds gathered in the sky. Lightning was fast approaching and ear-splitting thunder startled the little mermaid. The ship began to rock back and forth, and soon the waves seemed as high as mountains. They crashed into the deck so that the mermaid could no longer see the prince. Moments later, the ship was smashed to pieces and the little mermaid had to dodge the planks that showered down around her.

Just then, a flash of lightning lit up the scene and the little mermaid saw the prince plunge into the depths. She dived down and, when she found him, his body was limp and his eyes were closed—he was on the edge of life.

The little mermaid lifted him to the surface and let the waves carry them to a distant shore.

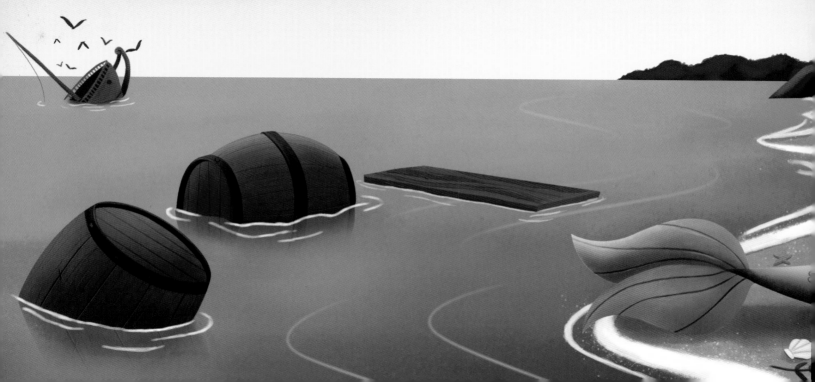

She laid the prince on the sparkling sands of a small bay and kissed him gently on the cheek. Then, she left him there and hid behind a rock, hoping that someone would find him.

Later in the morning, a pretty girl came down to the beach and found him lying there. The prince woke up and smiled at the girl, thanking her for saving him. The little mermaid was happy that he was safe, but sad that he didn't know who had really saved his life. She swam back to her father's palace feeling tired and troubled—she had fallen in love with the prince, and he didn't even know she existed.

For the next few weeks, the little mermaid was so unhappy, her sisters began to worry about her. Eventually, she told them her secret.

"I know where your prince lives!" said her eldest sister. "I've seen his palace. I'll take you there."

So the six sisters swam to the prince's palace, which stood white and shining by the sea. The little mermaid was so happy to see him. From that day, she swam outside his palace every night so she could catch a glimpse of the prince standing on his balcony.

Though she was overjoyed to see him, it wasn't enough—deep down, she yearned with all her heart to be human, just like him.

One day, she asked her grandmother whether it was possible. "Only if a human falls in love with you," she replied. "But that has never happened. They find our tails quite ugly, you see."

A tear rolled down the little mermaid's cheek. She knew she could never be happy if she didn't try to win the heart of her prince.

〜〜〜〜〜〜〜〜〜〜

That night, she swam secretly to the most fearsome place of all—the cavernous home of the Sea Witch.

Her heart beating wildly, she swam through bubbling whirlpools and eerie kelp forests, dodging venomous sea serpents and electric eels. When she finally reached the entrance to the cavern, the Sea Witch was already waiting for her.

"I've been expecting you," she said in a cold voice. "What you want will bring you only sorrow, but I will give it to you if you will give me a little something in return."

"What do you need?" asked the little mermaid, trembling.

"Your voice!" cackled the Sea Witch.

"But how will I tell the prince that it was I who saved him?"

"Not my problem!" said the Sea Witch. "You'll think of something."

And so the deal was done. The Sea Witch gave the little mermaid a potion and, in return, she gave her voice to the old crone.

"When you reach land," said the witch, "drink the potion and you will have human legs. But be warned—it hurts!"

The little mermaid swam away as fast as she could and, when she reached the shore by the prince's palace, she swallowed the foul-tasting potion. The transformation into a human was very painful, so painful that she passed out.

∿∿∿∿∿∿∿∿∿

When she woke, she found that she was being carried by the prince into the palace. Her heart skipped a beat.

He laid her down and asked who she was, but the poor mermaid couldn't reply—she had the human legs she longed for, but no voice. She looked at the prince with pleading eyes, but he didn't recognize her.

When she had recovered, she walked and danced so elegantly that the king and queen were sure that this mystery girl must be of royal blood. They sent messengers far and wide to discover the identity of the missing wordless princess, but they had no luck.

The little mermaid was treated well and became the prince's constant companion, but as she was unable to talk, she could never tell anyone her story—or truly win his heart.

A year went by and the little mermaid was still a mystery. With no proof that she was royal, the king and queen would never consider her a suitable bride for the prince, so they set out to find a love match for him. The little mermaid despaired to hear the news.

They soon set off on a voyage to meet the daughter of a nearby king. "She could never be as dear to me as you," said the prince to the little mermaid, and her heart swelled with hope again.

When they reached the shore of that faraway city, the king and his daughter stood waiting for them.

The princess was beautiful and looked strangely familiar. The little mermaid quickly realized that she was the girl who had found the prince washed up on the beach. The prince gasped, "It's you! You're the one who saved me!"

The little mermaid wanted to cry out, "No! I saved you, dear prince!" But not a sound passed through her lips.

She saw how the prince looked at the princess and knew that she saw true love in his eyes. The prince would never be hers. Her heart truly broken, she turned away to look at the sea.

At that moment, her five sisters popped up above the waves and beckoned her to come to them. The little mermaid knew then where she truly belonged, and she gracefully dived off the edge of the pier into the ocean, never to be seen by the prince again.

Rapunzel

Once upon a time, a man and his wife lived happily together but for one thing—they longed with all their hearts for a child. They were about to give up hope when the wife fell pregnant. They were happier than ever and could not wait for their precious baby to arrive.

The couple lived in a small house with no garden, but through the window, they could see into a walled garden, which was planted with fragrant herbs and juicy vegetables. It made their mouths water to see it, but nobody ever dared enter the garden, as it was owned by a most powerful sorceress.

The pregnant wife often gazed out of the window at the fresh green salad in the walled garden and wished that she could try it. In fact, she became so desperate to taste the salad that she couldn't eat anything else. The poor woman started to look pale and ill.

249

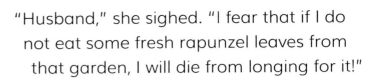

"Husband," she sighed. "I fear that if I do not eat some fresh rapunzel leaves from that garden, I will die from longing for it!"

The husband couldn't bear to lose his beloved wife, so he waited until dark, then he climbed over the wall to the garden, crept inside, and grabbed all the rapunzel leaves he could.

His wife craved the leaves so badly that, when he gave them to her, she ate them right away. However, instead of satisfying her craving, she found the rapunzel so delicious that she was desperate for more!

That night, once again, her husband braved the sorceress's garden to steal yet more rapunzel leaves. However, no sooner had he torn off the first leaf than the sorceress appeared before him. Her face was twisted with rage.

"Thief! How dare you break into my garden and steal my rapunzel!" she roared.

"Have mercy!" begged the man. "My pregnant wife saw your rapunzel from our window. She craved it so strongly, she thought she might die if she didn't try it!"

The sorceress's expression softened. "Very well," she said. "I will not punish you or your wife and you may help yourself to my rapunzel as often as you like, but on one condition—you must give up your child to me when it is born."

Terrified at the thought of the sorceress's punishment, the man agreed. And so, when a baby girl was born to the couple, the sorceress took the baby away.

They never again saw their daughter, but if they had, they would have seen what a lovely, thoughtful girl she turned out to be. The sorceress named her Rapunzel, after the leaves her mother had so craved.

Rapunzel grew to be a great beauty—she had big blue eyes and long, lustrous golden hair, which she plaited into neat braids.

Over time, the sorceress began to fear that someone would try to steal the girl away, so when Rapunzel turned twelve, the sorceress took her to the middle of the forest, where there stood a tall tower with no door and just a small window at the top. The tower was to be Rapunzel's new home and she was to live there all alone, where nobody could see her or find her.

The sorceress came to check on Rapunzel every day and, when she arrived, she would stand at the bottom of the tower and call out,

"Rapunzel, Rapunzel,
Let down your hair!"

When Rapunzel heard the sorceress's call, she would let her braids fall down to the ground, so that the sorceress could climb up them. And so this went on every day for many years.

Shortly after Rapunzel turned sixteen, she was sitting in her tower singing along with the birds, when a Prince came riding through the forest. The Prince heard Rapunzel's sweet voice and was completely enchanted by it. He circled the tall tower searching for an entrance, but he couldn't find one. Disappointed, he rode away but, that night, he couldn't stop thinking about the wonderful voice he had heard.

The next day he returned to the tower, but, as he drew near, he saw a strange lady in a purple robe walk up to it and shout out, "Rapunzel, Rapunzel! Let down your hair!"

A beautiful young lady appeared at the window and unwound long, golden braids, which the strange lady climbed. "Aha!" thought the Prince. "So that's the entrance to the tower!"

The Prince waited for the strange lady to leave, then he stood by the tower and called in a high voice, "Rapunzel, Rapunzel! Let down your hair!"

The same long golden braids fell to the ground and the Prince climbed up the tower. When he reached the top, Rapunzel was shocked to see him at her window. The Prince begged her forgiveness and explained that he had heard her singing and longed to meet her.

The two chatted all night. The Prince told Rapunzel all about his kingdom, and she told him of the sorceress who had kept her prisoner in the tower, and how she hoped to escape one day.

By morning, it was obvious that the pair had fallen in love. When the Prince asked Rapunzel to marry him, her heart was filled with happiness. But then she remembered that she had no means of escape.

However, Rapunzel came up with a plan. "Visit me every evening, after the sorceress has left, and bring with you some silk, then I can weave myself a ladder and escape!"

Gradually, Rapunzel's ladder got longer and stronger. But, one day, when Rapunzel was letting down her hair for the sorceress, she forgot herself and said, "How is it that you are so much more difficult to pull up than the Prince?"

Oh, how the sorceress shrieked! "You wicked girl!" she cried. "I kept you hidden away from the world and still you tricked me! Who is this Prince?"

Rapunzel wept and begged for kindness, but the sorceress conjured up some scissors and chopped off Rapunzel's long golden locks. Then, in a fit of anger and jealousy, she used her magic to banish Rapunzel to the wilderness.

That evening, when the Prince arrived at the tower, he called out and Rapunzel's golden braids cascaded to the ground as usual. However, when he reached the top, he found the sorceress waiting for him with a cruel look on her face.

"Your beautiful bird has flown away," she cackled. "You will never see her again!"

The sorceress leapt forward and pushed the poor heartbroken Prince out of the window, then used her magic to blind him. The Prince plummeted to the ground and, unable to see where he was going, he roamed the forest for days and then weeks, mourning the loss of Rapunzel.

Weeks turned into months and months turned into years, and the blind Prince walked the land, surviving on roots and berries, until one day, he walked into the very wilderness where Rapunzel had been abandoned by the sorceress.

It wasn't long before he heard a familiar voice singing a song he recognized, and he wandered in its direction with hope in his heart. Rapunzel looked up and saw her Prince walking to her. Crying tears of pure happiness, she ran to him, threw her arms around his neck and hugged him. As she did so, two tears rolled down her cheeks and fell into the Prince's eyes. All at once, the sorceress's evil spell was broken and he could see again!

The two set out on the long journey through the wilderness and forests back to the Prince's kingdom, where they were greeted with great joy and began a long and happy reign together—and they never saw the sorceress again.